# Twisted Sanity

# Twisted Sanity: Stories Beyond Reality

by
## Christopher Winterberg

ISBN-13: 978-0989448307
ISBN-10: 0989448304


Publisher: fu-X Publishing
Published date: June 2013


Cover Design and layout by Chris Wilke
Edited by Jacob Shaver
Printed in the United States of America

With sincere dedication, I would like to thank...you know who you are.

This book is dedicated to the one person who took my writing seriously enough to believe in what I was doing and who sent my writing in the right direction with her critique of my first works. You're more trusted and admired than you'll ever know. And you are the one who taught me to speak soulfully and listen attentively. You said, "I believe in you."

## Acknowledgements

I would like to thank my family and friends for the continual support and encouragement to press forward with my writing. I would also like to thank all those who beta read my stories and offered changes, whether structural, copy edit, or just said, " Hey, this kinda sucks. Change it."

# Table of Contents

**A Bizarre Future**
Did you know using a credit card could get you shot?
Home ownership is in life's plot.
With witty banter, I said "no."
Big Box savings and zombies moving slow.

# Debt Solution

"Hello. My name is Carla from The Large Charge Card Company. Is Mr. Larry Larson available?" she asked while looking at the sheet to make sure she had the correct name.

"This is Larry."

"Hello, Mr. Larson. How are you today?"

"Fine?" He said, but it came out more as a question. He was a bit confused why his credit card people would be calling him.

"Sir, I am calling you regarding your credit card account."

"Okay. Did something happen?" he asked, still a bit nervous that maybe someone had stolen his identity.

"Sir, nothing has happened with your account and that is exactly why I'm calling you."

"Uh. I'm sorry. I don't understand," he said with a pause.

"Sir, your payment was due yesterday by midnight and it is now the next day..."

Larry immediately cut in, "Wait a second! My payment didn't make it to you yesterday by midnight so you're calling me now? It's 11:00 AM the next day. That's less than twelve hours after it was due. Are you kidding me?"

"Sir, I am not kidding you. I do not joke about missed payments."

"Seriously! Here, I'll pay it now. Are you ready?" He asked her as he reached for his checkbook for his routing number.

"Sir, unfortunately your payment will be late whether I take your payment or not. Do you understand?"

"Well, uh, yeah, I get that, but I'll just pay now."

"Sir, that is fine; however, it will still be late. That fact cannot be changed; therefore, the agreement that you signed before taking control of your account will be in effect. That means that the penalties *must* be carried out."

"Must? Hold on a goddamn second! What penalties?"

"Sir, please do not use vulgarity on the phone. Thank you. I will briefly explain the missed payment penalties that you fully agreed to when you signed your cardholder agreement with LCCC: Missed payments are an unforgivable offense, completely, utterly, and disgustingly unforgivable. Just one and LCCC takes control of unsecured material assets. Do you understand?" she said it in a straight-through manner without a breath.

"Uh-huh, um, not really. Here's my bank information."

"Sir, I do apologize, but that will have to wait until after I finish with the penalties. A second offense and a reminder will be sent with The Cut Squad. They come for a finger. Three and it is a toe, the big one. By the fifth, we castrate males and pluck the ovaries from females. Do— —you——understand?"

"Yeah, that's a good one," he said with a soft, but plainly nervous chuckle. "Sir, I am very serious."

"What about age?" he said with that chuckle getting longer and louder. "Age does not matter. We just take, period."

Still laughing a bit, "Well, you never mentioned what happens on the very first late payment."

"Sir, what material items did you purchase in the past thirty days?"

"Um, I'm...what?"

"Sir, what material items did you purchase in the past thirty days?"

"Uh, what exactly do you mean?" he asked shaking his head, even though he knew Carla could not see him.

"Okay, sir, the easiest way to explain it is to ask

2

you what material items did you purchase in the past thirty days?" she asked, irritated.

"Hmmmm. Material? I guess that'd be the Big Screen LCD, a lounger chair, and well, this phone I'm talking to you on right now," he said, not really caring, while peeking around the corner of his kitchen wall to check-in on his precious plasma princess. The screen was vivid with deep, rich colors and he could see it clearly from any angle.

"Sir, that's great. I'll dispatch a unit to get those things immediately. They'll be there within the hour."

"Oh. Oka...WAIT! What? What the hell...?"

She interrupted him after his swear word, "Sir, there is no need to holler and cuss."

"What? Someone's coming to take my, MY things?"

"Sir, technically those items have not been paid for, so therefore they belong to the Large Charge Card Company. We thank you for your purchases," she added spryly.

"No! No-no! No! You can't just come to my house and take those things. NO! I'm not letting anyone take those things!"

"Sir, according to the cardholder agreement you signed, we have the right of ownership to any material items you purchased from your last payment to your missed payment. It's written in section N, subsection D-26, paragraph 112, sentence 93 of catalog one. Would you like me to read it to you?"

"No! That will not be necessary because I'm not giving my..." he paused as he heard a knock at the door. "Oh, c'mon. Seriously? They're at my front door? No fuuuchk...uh, sorry, fudgin' way! I'm not lettin' 'em in?"

"Sir, I strongly suggest that you allow them to enter your premises."

"Or what? What are they gonna do, break down my

3

door?" he said with a snicker while suspiciously looking at his front door.

"Sir, according to section P, subsection A-6, paragraph 5, sentence 19 of book three of your cardholder agreement, Large Charge Card Company has the legal right to enter the cardholder's household, place of business, or anything that is owned or holds the cardholder's recently purchased material items. LCCC can, by any means necessary, enter the household. Would you like me to read it to you?"

"What! No! No way! I never read that crap! Who the hell reads all that anyway?"

"Sir, the very first page of our cardholder agreement *catalogs* clearly states that the cardholder *must* read all the fine print. It is written plainly in six-point font in order to reduce paper and combine everything into three encyclopedia-sized catalogs instead of five or six. Contrary to popular belief, we are environmentally friendly and do not attempt to trick people. Everything is written in the agreement. Everything. Did you read it?" She said it all in a flurry.

"Sir? She paused and waited, but heard nothing. "Sir? Sir, are you there?"

"Uh, yeah, sure. I'm here. Are you a robot?"

"Sir, no, I am not a robot."

"Look, I'm gonna have to hang up because they're packing up my TV and chair.

I'm sure they'll grab my phone next." His voice trailed off on the last few words. "Sir, are you okay? I could barely hear you."

"No. No, I'm not. I'm not really okay."

"Sir, what's wrong?"

"Besides that I might be having a stroke, nothing really. Oh yeah, THEY'RE TAKING MY STUFF! MY STUFF!"

"Sir, there is absolutely no need to yell. Are you

having a stroke or do you require medical assistance?"

"No. No I do not require medical assistance." He remarked snidely while grinding his teeth.

"Sir, just as a reminder, if you need medical assistance and are unable to pay your medical expenses, we do offer an extremely low-rate medical card, The Medium Medical Card. Granted, it's not nearly as big as The Large Charge Card, but it can help pay those pesky medical bills. Shall I assist you with the process of applying now?" she asked cheerfully.

"Apply? Will it bring my TV and chair back?" He asked sarcastically.

"Sir, I'm sorry. No it will not. But, it will come in handy if you miss a second or third payment." She said, a smile on her face. Larry could feel it through the phone.

He was at the point where he could actually feel his blood pressure rise. He felt that if he looked in the mirror, which was paid for, that he'd see smoke coming from his ears just like in the cartoons. He was that pissed off and he really couldn't understand how Carla remained so calm under *his* tension. He finally realized that it was her job to make him upset by spewing a dose of reality and he fell for it. She had spun the web and he was trapped. He struggled to wriggle free, but he could not escape the black widow that was the LCCC.

Thinking he developed an idea to beat the all-too-large conglomerate, "So it's only after the *first* missed payment that you take my, uh, any *unpaid* material purchases?"

"Sir, that is correct; however, be advised what occurs as future non-payment penalties."

"Oh, I am. I'm very aware. I'll call you back, and Carla, may I call *you* specifically?"

"Sir, I am sorry but our system is set as such that your next incoming call will be answered randomly. There is a seventeen percent chance that I could possibly receive your call. Will that be all, sir?"

"In that case, Carla, lets start that medical card application thing." He said with a light, but nervous laugh as he watched his cherished television being carried out his front door. He lowered his head and whispered a silent goodbye. *Until we meet again, my dear.*

# What You See

"Mr. Miller, please sign here," Mary said while pointing to the line highlighted in yellow, "and then please sign right here," again she pointed. "Okay, Mr. Miller, I promise you this is the last signature needed," and with that she pointed the ballpoint pen to the last line on the contract. "Well, that's it Mr.,"

"Ya know, just call me Jerry," the man immediately interrupted the real estate agent.

"Congratulations, Jerry! You are now a new home owner,"

Jerry noticed as she gently slid the house keys across the cherry wood-finished tabletop. He noticed the key chain as the silver finish caught the overhead lighting and threw a brief sparkle in the air. It was as if the keys were saying, "Here we are, Jerry. Take us!"

Jerry had looked at too many houses to remember. It came down to the quaint three bedrooms and two bathrooms with the refreshing pool in the spacious backyard or the four bedrooms and three bathrooms with a small enough yard to trim with a weed trimmer alone and no pool or garage. He opted for the relaxing backyard oasis and a safe place to park his car and motorcycle. The house at 4666 Lucas Lane was now his.

Three days later, and after the fresh paint had dried, the movers arrived with all of Jerry's possessions. He was like a traffic officer, directing people every which way as boxes were unpacked and furniture was moved into his new home. Boxes were brought in and Jerry looked around and a feeling of previously being in the house washed over him. He felt like he belonged.

It wasn't just the feeling of viewing the house on two previous occasions before his purchase. He had the feeling that he had maybe been in the house once many years ago. Jerry shook it off as just the newness of home ownership.

That first night Jerry unpacked all the small boxes and placed things were he felt they should go for the time being. It was a long day and Jerry was happy to head to bed.

The previous owners left behind only one thing. It hung in the entranceway of the front foyer. It was a generously sized wall mirror with a dark mahogany finish outlined in warm brown tones. Jerry ran his hand over the accented beveled edges and along the rounded top. *Hmm, strong and sturdy to the eye. I like it. Keep it, Jerry. Keep it.* Intricately carved log branches and oak leaves, done by hand, provided a sophisticated, but rugged design touch. *Put it in the bedroom. It'll be perfect and close to you other things.* He carefully took it down and heaved it on a wall in the master bedroom.

Jerry woke up late the next morning. With not much to do but finish his move and meet some friends, he thought sleep would do him well. It was just after eleven when He was out of the shower and dressed to leave. As he buttoned his shirt, he walked over to his newly hung mirror to see how he looked. "Lookin' good Jer!" he said out loud to his reflection as he made the hand gesture of a shooting pistol.

Just as Jerry picked up his foot to move away, he spotted something in the lower corner of the mirror. He looked closer and saw two people off in the distance, yet they remained in the mirror. He threw a confused look over his shoulder and saw nothing. His gaze came back to the mirror and there they were.

He paid attention to the people and saw a man with a mask over his face slowly pulling a lady. He had one hand over her nose and mouth and the other under her arm and across her chest as he pulled her against her will. She was dragged with her legs splayed and fighting every inch as her heels pounded the carpet. She clutched a small gray leather bag in her hand. *Shit! Shit! Shit! It's happening, Jer. The doc said it'd happen and it's happening. Fuck! The meds. Take the meds. Goddammit, take the meds!*

Jerry spun his head again to look behind him and saw nothing. He peered into the mirror and the image was gone. Jerry could feel his pulse quicken and his stomach tighten. He shook his head to clear the image away. "Holy shit Jer, I think ya need to lay off the Vicodin, dude," he mumbled before walking off. Jerry was on medication for a knee pain that just would not go away. It was a gift from his time in the Army. Jerry surmised that he'd been under a lot of stress with the move and he was obviously hallucinating.

*What the fuck? Take 'em or lay off 'em? I'm not a doctor. Call the doctor. Should I? What if...nah. Could it be...? I mean, was that me in the mirror? Of course, you idiot. It was you. It's a fucking mirror, asshole. Who else would it be? Christ, you're an idiot.*

Jerry arrived at the bar to meet his football buddies and watch his team. During the game, Jerry's mind wandered to what he had seen earlier. He just couldn't manage to shake it. With three seconds left, his team kicked a game-winning field goal to make the playoffs, but Jerry was buzzed from a six-pack and another two pain pills that he barely realized what had happened.

Back at his home, Jerry immediately ran to his room and searched the mirror for any sign of what had terrorized him earlier that day. He saw nothing but his dumb reflection staring back. He angrily stomped off and went to bed. Drunk and high from medication, Jerry passed out almost as soon his head hit the pillow.

He woke at five o'clock shaking the impending hangover from his aching head. He reached for the water from his nightstand and then tapped his touch lamp to give light to the corner of his room. Two massive gulps

9

of refreshment and Jerry was over to the mirror, staring quizzically. "Give it to me! Show me something! Come on!" Jerry talked to the mirror like it was another person. He saw a blurry figure moving in the bottom corner of the glass. He made out the masked man holding his hands above his head in a teepee formation. Something was in his hands, but he couldn't make it out.

Looking over his shoulder, he reassured himself that he was alone and then searched the mirror for the mystery image. He saw Mr. Mask holding an object and moving slowly. "Whatchya got there, friend?" Jerry asked the mirror, waiting for the answer. He made out a flat-looking, shiny image.

He realized that it was an ax blade and saw that the man was about to drive it down into the head of a seated woman, her hands bound behind her back with brown corded rope. It was like he was watching a grainy black-and-white film. Blood shot sideways as Jerry turned away and covered his eyes.

"What the hell!" Jerry shouted while his eyes searched excitedly. His heart pounded with every heavy breath. He scurried back to his bed, and like a little kid, pulled the covers over his head for safety. He curled up into a fetal position and rocked to ease his nerves. After about thirty minutes and feeling a bit safer, Jerry reached his hand out from beneath the sanctuary of his blanket hideout to grab his pill and some water. As the medication made its way down Jerry's swollen throat, he thought that maybe it was the prescription that was making him see things.

It was almost ten in the morning when Jerry woke up for the second time. First he peeked above the comfy confines of his blanket enclosure. Then his eyes ran past the mirror to the French doors. His eyes continued to the bathroom arch and over to his dresser. His eyes came full circle to his nightstand and fixed on his hands clasping to the cashmere coverlet offering him protection.

Like a little girl being told she was pretty, Jerry took his eyes toward the ground at the side of his bed and brought them back up, staring at the evil, hanging on the wall. In robotic motion, like he was under a trance, he slowly lifted his covers and climbed out of the warmth of his bed. He methodically walked to the mirror. "Talk to me. Tell me who *he* is. Tell me dammit!" Jerry's voice was pleading, and authoritative.

He caught the glimpse of the masked assailant staring back at him. The man was holding a knife and walking toward Jerry. Jerry spun on his heels and leaned back. There was no one there. His eyes quickly scanned the entire room. No one. Demanding answers, Jerry turned aggressively to the wall and placed his hands on the sides of the frame. "Enough! Who are you?" He shouted. "I'm losing it. Now I'm talking to a goddamn mirror AND myself. Holy shit, I need Dr. Damascus."

There he was, the image. The killer appeared again, holding the knife. Jerry watched as he walked at a fast pace. He sped up as he approached a lady wearing a pink floral hat. He placed one hand over her mouth while taking the knife slowly and deliberately along her neck and pulling it through gracefully like playing a violin bow along the string. Blood trickled and then sprang from the victim as her body gradually crumpled to the ground.

Jerry began to tremble and to sweat profusely. He had an anxious feeling that brought about brief pangs of hunger. He knew better than to eat. He sat on the side of his bed and placed his head in his hands and wept.

It was almost noon and Jerry decided to call Dr. Damascus after lunch. Jerry went into the bathroom and washed the sweat from his face. He never looked in the mirror out of straight-laced fear. He kept his head down and walked into the closet to unpack a few more items from those pesky boxes seemingly laughing at him. *One down, two to go,* he thought.

Jerry gently dug around and picked through his packed belongings. He placed a few things on the shelf and threw some dress shoes in the corner. He reached for the last box and the tape peeled off in one single strip. Jerry reached in and took out another smaller box and gently placed in on the top shelf, but nearer to the corner and in the back.

Later that day Jerry's friend, Melissa, came over to help with his unfinished unpacking and organizing. Jerry liked her, but Melissa made it too clear to Jerry that the two were only friends. They did a lot together: hiking, dinners, events, movies, and just hanging out – he trusted her and felt comfortable with her.

She knew many of his secrets. She would talk to him about her boyfriends and what assholes they ended up being after she got to know them. On this day, she was there for Jerry. When she walked in the door, he noticed a large onyx ring on her finger.

"Nice! Is it new?" Jerry asked, pointing silver band.

"Yup! Bought it yesterday as a gift to myself," she said with a grin.

Melissa went straight to work helping Jerry get things in proper places and he trusted that she knew where things would look best. She knew so well that she decided that certain items should be packed back up for good.

"Uh, Jer, I don't think you *really* need to have this collection of miniature football helmets prominently displayed on your center table."

"Hmm. Well? Uh, okay." He wanted to defend the display; however, he knew she was right and there was no way past it.

"And, do you *really* want this stuffed deer head on *this* wall? I think it might look better, oh, I don't know, out of the main living space." She said it with such fervor and vigor that the sarcasm was well hidden.

"Are you movin' in or somethin'?" Jerry said half laughing, but realizing again, she was right. "How would it look in my study?"

"Yeah, that's a good place for it," she yelled from the living room. "Right in the garbage can in your study," she mumbled with disbelief, while shaking her head that he even owned such a thing.

Melissa scooped up the mini helmet collection and used her shirt as a storage source and headed for the back room toward Jerry.

"Hey, ya got an empty box for these?"

"Sure, top shelf in the master closet."

As Melissa walked past him, through the bathroom and into the closet, it hit Jerry that the box was not quite empty and an awkward feeling coursed through him. He hesitated, raised his head, looked toward Melissa and slowly walked to the closet.

Melissa had found the box and began to remove the lid. Peering inside, she slowly turned and looked up at Jerry.

"This is some weird stuff."

"Sorry," he quietly mumbled.

Later in the day, Jerry looked at that same box and then reached for it. He ripped the lid off like he was tearing open a birthday present. Relieved to see that the items inside were still in place, ho took a long deep breath. The pink golf hat, his lucky brown rope, and the small gray travel bag were all still in the box. He dropped in a small black and silver object, placed the lid back and headed toward the phone.

Before calling Dr. Damascus, Jerry walked past the mirror: He stopped and lifted his head high, while peering directly down past his nose and glared at the mirror, never hesitating, never wavering, and squinted and raised the corner of his upper lip.

13

"Fuck you!" He blurted in a raspy cigarette-laden voice, while spit spewed from his pursed lips and splattered on the glass. He reached for the phone, but not without one last yell to his mirror, "Damn you! Damn you to hell! You don't know the truth! You see, but you'll never know why. Never!"

The mirror knew his face. It saw his crimes. It knew what haunted him. He had nightmares, incredibly lucid, vivid nightmares. He tried to forget, but the mirror would not allow it.

Jerry dropped the receiver, stammering to the closet. Reaching for the box, tossing back the cover, he grabbed the ring. Placing it on his right ring finger, he went sauntering to the mirror. Leaning in, throwing a hard right cross, the black onyx crashed into and shattered the glass. The cut on his hand sent blood oozing and dripping onto the carpet, staining and creating a pooling effect.

*There! Happy now? Asshole. Idiot. Why don't you like me? Huh? Why? Now she's gone. They're all gone. Gone! You bastard! Like me! Just like me...once...please.* He knelt, peering into the shattered glass. He reached, smearing his hand in the bloody mess, bringing his hand to his face, he wiped. He lurched for the long, thin chard, grabbing it so tight his left hand dripping blood, he brought it to his neck.

# The Reversal

I'm not interested. I gave at the office, I tell him. He's persistent and quite a pain-in-the-ass. "Don't you care about the kids? It's for the children." His subtle tactic is an attempt to reach for my softer, more sympathetic side. Little does he know that I'm a granite rock, immovable, rough, and hard-as-hell.

Some kid slashed my tires last week. Fuck those little bastards I say and slam the phone down. It's obvious that my adrenaline has taken over, my pulse has quickened, and I need to sit down. No more than ten minutes has passed and just as I'm going through my air-boxing scene from Rocky, the phone rang.

Look, I asked you to stop calling me. "Sir, you never asked me to stop calling. You only hung up on me." Good point I mention and then proceed to ask him to stop calling. "But, sir, it's the holiday season and the children's charity could use the extra support, especially this time of the year," he argues. Another good point, but I definitely do not tell him that.

I'm not interested in kids. Don't have any and certainly don't want any. And as far as support goes, when the hell is someone gonna realize that we simply can't support every damn person in the world? What about people in this country? What about kids *here*? It's rhetorical, no need to answer I tell him. I go on with my rant for a few minutes longer until I hear the unwanted and awkwardness of complete silence. It's the conversational equivalent of a galactic black hole. Suddenly I feel as though my only audience is, well, just me. Hello. Hello. Hey! Hello? Then, there it is, the almighty throttling and despairing click on the other end.

I feel empty inside. I feel lonely. I feel despair. I feel vulnerable. I feel afraid. "Did he just hang up on *me*?" I ask myself out loud. Again, those feelings make

15

me feel uneasy. I need to sit. No, I should stand. I begin to pace, looking at the phone waiting for it to ring. Nothing. I think for a moment.

This is ridiculous. Was my commentary oblivious to the real question? Was it perceived as fact or opinion? Did he find my haranguing impudent? Did I overreach? Doesn't he like me? Why do I care? I do care. Who am I to speak for the masses? I rarely even speak for myself. I do care. Maybe it wasn't kids who slashed my tires. Maybe it was those guys I saw walking that dog the other night. Yeah, it must have been them. Wait, why would two guys walk a dog...unless, they're...no, they don't look it. How do I know what *it* looks like anyway?

I pause for a second, only briefly though, to wonder where I lost him in the phone conversation. When did he stop listening and did he stop or just switch me off on his headset? Guess it was more than a quick second. All right, it was several. I do care! Dammit!

I pick up the phone and hit the recall button

# A Love Story

I was working the night shift on a Saturday at the local warehouse store, you know, the big-box retailer that came in and pushed out all the little guys. I mean, it's the largest store known to humankind. I raise my arms wide open for visual effect. We would use binoculars to see from one end to the other. The place was open twenty-four hours a day, seven days a week, and three hundred and sixty-five days a year. No closing. No sleeping. Never!

I am the second assistant manager and I was working with Sheila, Shellie, Sheryl, and the night manager, Sherlock. They were all related. The three girls were triplets and Sherlock was their older brother, the Shaffer foursome.

Before you ask, yes, some parent, or parents, actually named their kid Sherlock. It wasn't a nickname because he was smart or a moniker he was gifted for any keen sleuth- solving skills. It was his everyday-name: Sherlock Shelton Shaffer.

So, like I was saying, I was working with the four of them. My shift ended at two in the morning, and as luck would have it, it just so happened that Shellie was done working at the exact same time I was. I mean, what were the odds of that happening? It happened because I love her.

I wall-flowered near the only operating checkout lane until I could see her charmful beauty strolling down aisle one toward the front automatic doors and I magically appeared as she approached. I envisioned her in one of those rock videos from the 1980s - the ones where her hair would be blowing from the breeze while she was in high heels and leather.

Even though we never closed, we did lock some sets of doors for safety reasons. I had to unlock those

17

doors to leave, and as the second assistant manager, I had keys, so waiting was necessary. It was necessary, too, because, well, I love her. I nonchalantly smile. *Idiot idiot idiot. Dumbass dumbass dumbass*. I tell myself because I could have smiled so much better.

We walk out to the extremely lit parking lot together. That's what I call being about ten feet apart. It's a start. She is silent, but listening to me as I jabber about the past shift. There are four cars in the lot and I only count that there should be three, hers, Sherlock's, and mine. I stop her for a moment to assess the situation. And, well, because I love her. I start out by telling her not to look and ask her if it seems strange that there is a suspicious car in the lot. She thinks I'm weird. She looks.

I look at my Time-ex watch to note that Officer Rodgers should be coming along any second on his Segway. Yes, the watch is actually a *genuine* knockoff of the real thing. Got it in New York on the street in Times Square. Rodgers is our outside security and sure to the minute, he zips past, off in the distance. If he's not worried, I'm not worried I tell her. *Dummy dummy dummy!* I could hit myself.

She looks at me, probably disgusted, but probably not, and tells me good night. I watch her walk away to her car. Wait! I sorta yell, but it was late and dark so it came out wispy and nasally in a nervous kinda way. I point to *the* car.

It was rolling, but in a herky-jerky way like when a kid first learns to drive a stick and has issues with the clutch sequence. It stops about twenty feet from my car and the lights go off. Then the horn blasts and blares for about ten seconds. I didn't time it, but I could have. Shellie moves towards me and we both look at the car. I can smell her lotion. Fresh like flowers. I love her.

We just stand there, by the side of my car, looking and waiting. I decide enough is enough. I saunter out from behind my protective cover, careful not to alarm whoever, whomever, I always confuse the two, is in the car. I look back and offer a soft nod to Shellie, mostly because I loved her, but also to comfort her. Because I love her.

Suddenly the driver rolls, yes, rolls, as in manually, down the window. Smoke bellows out and I can instantly smell the aroma of the weed. I cautiously step closer to see a man driving, well not anymore, but he's sitting in the seat, and a woman in the other. The door opens and he steps out. I step back, about five feet back. I go all the way back to my car.

He just stood there like he was in shock. Probably because he was stoned too. His clothes were a bit dingy and tattered, his hair was unkempt, and the smell, we could smell him from thirty feet. Shellie grabbed my arm, lightly, but with enough pressure that suggested you're my man, "Do something." I was her hero too.

"Where are your sisters and Sherlock?" I ask calmly, feigning interest so she'll see me as a caring and compassionate sweetheart of a guy. And, because I love her.

"Break room," she quickly answers, then shooing me with her hand to go do something.

Right now I hate absolutely everything about Shellie except that I absolutely love everything about her. That complicates things. We've been dating for almost three weeks now. Well, that's what I call making sure I take my break at the exact same time she does every day. She calls it creepy. I almost asked her out, once, but I walked past without even a simple smile. Now though, we're entrenched in a soon-to-be battle for all mankind right here in my city.

As I peer into the dimly lit space in front of me, it's clear to me that he's...he's a real life, true-to-me, living zombie. Well, not *actually* living, of course. I do not see him as a threat. His smell, yes, him, no.

We deftly maneuver toward the trunk of my car, being careful not to be seen. Zombie number one, I called him Ed, did not move. His tongue lolled out of his mouth, similar to that of an exhausted dog, but Ed was standing trying to reach at the side mirror. He had a large bite on his outstretched arm, maybe by a dog or another zombie. I don't know - do zombies even bite each other? I wasn't sure. Probably not, but maybe if they're hungry. I made a mental note to ask if I got the chance.

I look at the guy; his skin is pale, dark, and blotchy. I know that pale and dark are a contradiction, but you weren't there. They were both at the same time. He has blistery things on his face and neck and he appears to have a severe limp as he tries to walk towards us. He swings around in a quick, but obvious way, as the passenger door opens.

I can see that he is missing his right arm and suddenly that explains the spasmodic driving. No wonder, I say to Shellie. She looks at me in disgust, probably, but probably not. I amble out from behind my car again and then confidently walk towards the gentleman.

"Welcome to...!" I say in a high-pitched voice. And after hearing it I stop mid- sentence.

"Why'd you say that?" Shellie asks in a sharp tone unbecoming of a girlfriend.

"I don't know! I'm nervous! We say it to all our customers." That squeaky pitch is back.

"Shhh! Don't yell." She says as she lightly touches my arm. She loves me.

"Sorry! Nervous." I blather. *Stupid stupid stupid stupid* is all I can think to myself as I could have said so many other cooler things to her at that zombierific moment. "Trey, there's a finger over there, next to the walkway!" Shellie blurts and points out. And then in an excited voice, "A finger, Trey! A finger!"

"I'm on it!" I say as I take off, staying low like a running back, not really realizing what I just heard, and then quickly slow to a light jog as I see that she meant the other walkway, not the one on my immediate right. I'm no Olympian, but I'm in shape. Maybe not good enough shape for Shellie, but who really cares. I do. I love her.

For whatever reason, and not fully understanding why, I scoop up the finger and I place the digit in the pocket of my blaze orange safety vest. It's basically the store uniform, except mine says second assistant manager. I take off for the car, staying low, of course. I'm not sure why - because the zombie, uh, Ed, wasn't looking anyway. I wasn't fully sure if zombies could see or not. Mental note number two.

Just as I arrive at the trunk, Shellie's lovely voice is in my ear again, "Holy crap! There's an arm over there!"

"A whole arm?" I jokingly ask while absorbing what I just did and with my back leaning against the car like I'm in a violent shootout, except I'm not.

"Well, at least halfa arm."

"I'm on it!" I tell her, half outta breath, but loving her nonetheless, from my run. As the second assistant manager, I take it upon myself, for whatever reason, to maintain a clean parking lot.

I spot the forearm lying on the ground next to a load-bearing pole for shopping cart return. I can only surmise that whoever, whomever, lost it must've hit that pole pretty hard. I grab the arm and take off carrying it like a grayish, rotten steak of a football, cradling it in-between my elbow and cupped hand. I feel like OJ running through the airport in that commercial, again, staying low. I'm not even sure where the hell I'm headed anymore when I hear Shellie's angelic voice, "Over here, dufus. D-u-f-u-s, here!" She shouts in a low voice pointing at the ground next to her as if I'm a dog and should come happily. I accept the pet name. I love her.

21

I see, out of the corner of my eye, Rodgers' Segway lying on its side in the yellow painted crosswalk of the empty lot. I turn to tell Shellie to tell her we should make a run for it, but she is already gone. I attempt to approach Ed once again only this time I have his arm. Well, half his arm anyway.

I walk slowly, holding the forearm in both hands out in front of me as a peace offering with my arms extended, being careful not to irk him in any way. I ask him how he's doing, but he only looks at me with a slight head tilt and stoner eyes. I tell him I have brought his arm back to him and not to eat me. He doesn't seem hungry so I continue. I am close enough that his stench feels like it is jumping from him to me. I take one deep breath and reach out his departed limb to him. Again, he does nothing. My moment is now.

In one swift motion, I not so gently, but strategically, lodge his right forearm back into the hole where it once grew. He seems happy. We could be friends, if he doesn't eat me. I back away slowly, watching Ed the entire time. I feel the presence of eyes on me so I turn, slowly as to not scare Ed.

"Hey!" I shout in a low and unassuming, as not to alarm Ed, but steady and manly, voice. "Wait up." Shellie cruises up on the rolling transporter, stops on a dime and spins, as her long vibrant blonde locks flow in the breeze she has created. It's like she's a commercial. I stare at her elegance and beauty. I love her.

"Dufus! Hey, d-u-f-u-s!" She yells out slowly enough to pull me from my love- induced trance. She always had that term of endearment for me. "Get on. Let's go!"

We zip down a ways and then hear a thunderous crash. "It's coming from Outdoor and Garden." I tell her. "We should foot it from here. We're already close." This was Shellie's fourth week and she was still getting to know the lay of the land. I was the second assistant manager so I knew where most things were.

We peer from around the cinderblock corner of the building, but see nothing. We are side-by-side, creeping into the tree section of Outdoors. I eyeball the area as we crouch next to a small Yucca tree. We peek from the end of the adjoining aisle, between the boxes of fertilizer and flathead shovels, to see a man standing in front of a knocked over outdoor barbecue glass-door refrigerator.

That display model was part of our new childproof appliance section. We used a standard latch-and-hook lock attached with adhesive. I helped with the display and we ran outta the regular sticky backing so I grabbed an industrial strength type from automotive. Apparently it worked very well, maybe too well. I was pleased with myself. He stood there with the broken handle in his hand.

Shellie whispers in my ear that he is missing a finger. The softness of her breath is like a warm and gentle sunshiny breeze on a lazy summer morning. I love her. The zombie looked a lot like Mr. Rodgers and eventually walked off without his digit. We decide to run back to the parking lot. By the time we get around the corner, Sheila, Sheryl, and Sherlock were outside staring in awe at the zombies in the lot.

We watched as Ed and his zombified lady, I called her Vivian, walked arm-in-arm off into the night by the light of the full moon. Looks like that arm is holding up pretty good I mention to Shellie. She seems disgusted, probably, but probably not.

"Would you like to go to dinner sometime? With me?" I ask her nervously. "What?" She asked sharply, still looking into the darkness of the zombified night. "Shellie would you like to go to dinner with me?" I ask in a more formal way, but still nervous.

"I'm Sheila." She says with a sharp eyebrow raised.

23

Not wanting to lose any previously built momentum in our relationship, I unhesitatingly smile, "Of course you are. I know that. It was a test to see if you were traumatized."

She offers a lazy smile, almost contrived at best, probably because she loathes me, "Yes. Yes I would." Sheila and I have been through more than most on our short relationship tour, but I love her.

"Zombies?" Sherlock asks, pointing into nowhere but the darkness of the night.

"No shit, Sherlock." It's all I could get out between deep breaths with my hands on my waist.

Sheila and I walk off to the car, together. You can never really plan for zombies I tell her. They just happen. You look once and nothing. Look again and a guy with one leg dragging beside him is making his way toward you with a half eaten brain dripping from his hand.

I never did ask Ed my zombie questions, but that doesn't matter now. I saved my city. I saved it because of Shellie or Sheila. Doesn't really matter which one because, well, I love her.

### Sleep Well My Sweet
Something's abuzz, but will it kill you tonight?
Lying in wait, quiet, and out of sight.
Darkness falls and a hitchhiker lost on a trek.
Hats, writing, and needles—a pain in the neck.

# Buzz Kill

I hear the buzz. Patiently I waited. I waited for the landing. The little bastard figured out how to avoid the warmth of life that the light offers him. He has conquered his fear of ultimate darkness. He flies overhead just far enough away so I must twist and turn to hear for his location. I perk an ear here. I perk an ear over that way. Nothing.

I know he's there. He's always there. "Fuck you." I whisper into the darkness of night. I'm fidgety. I feel things that aren't there. Zzzzzzz, past one ear and then past the other. "Oh hell! Just get me already!" It's been said the anticipation is worse than the event and I think he knows it. He's a master of illusion, a tactician of timeliness, and a champion of bravado.

He knows just when and where to strike. *Maybe it's my ozone-loving carbon footprint-reducing CFL bulb? Is that why he has no need to approach the glorious light? Is he immune to the CFL? What is CFL again? Is his microscopic ameba-size brain smarter than any human?*

Those questions I pondered with my touch lamp at arm's length. I searched the ceiling and steadily brought my gaze down the wall in a fixed concentration. It's him or me. "Where are you now, shithead? Show yourself!"

He's up there, somewhere, perched and getting ready. Like a cougar prowling in the unknown he will appear when I cannot see him. I'll be defenseless against his Kamikaze attack. Perhaps his throne sits atop the curtain? Maybe he's in the corner, motionless and ready to launch his bloodthirsty strike at first darkness? Maybe he's sitting at the corner of my nightstand readying his disease-laden hypodermic needle of a stinger, preparing to plunge the syringe deep into my cushy flesh?

In an attempt to coax him into my world of sight, I turn out the light, with my finger at the ready to bring the light blazing back. His blood-drunk quest shall begin shortly. The buzz is distant, and then suddenly, with fierce precision he shot like a torpedo toward the warmth of my head.

I swatted like King Kong, but had the accuracy of a bull in the losing effort. "Your time will come you little shit!" I blurted in dismay at missing him completely and coming ever nearer to actually hitting myself.

The clock ticked slowly in the battle and my eyes grew weary as my body, exhausted, begged to begin its descent into sleep. I breathed deep and exhaled long. I repeated as my yoga had taught me. My instructor always said that I should get something out of my practice. "Take it with you," she would softly instruct with the fingertips of each hand touching ever so slightly. Little did she know I'd take those necessary breathing techniques straight to the killing field of my personal war against life or death.

I felt the melting sensation of full relaxation. I became very tranquil and my right arm twitched in approval of drifting off. Then, without any form of warning, there it was, I felt a tick on my face.

Now fully awake, heart racing, after I slapped myself, the buzz was ever clear. He almost got me! A nanosecond from disaster, but a bite-free red lumpless face to show my victory, the light went back on.

I scanned my immediate area as my eyes reached out into the hazy distance. I saw nothing. I ventured from the cozy comfy confines of my bed and scanned some more. He was lurking, waiting. He bided his time laughing behind my back, to my face, and all around me. He's a shifty sort with Ninja reflexes and F-16 speed; a deadly combination.

My game is power; pure unadulterated, hate-fueled, rage-ridden, man-against-the- world power.

I would stop at no end to rest in peace on that

beautiful night. I succumbed to the fact that I would only get three hours of sleep, but it would be a glorious and peaceful three hours.

Along the journey of a potentially sleepless night, I went through the five stages of grief. I reached denial immediately. Perplexed, not knowing or caring why the unseen flyer wanted me, my mind wandered. *Perhaps it was after someone else? No! No one else lives in the house! Maybe, just maybe he was in the wrong spot? Did he have the right address?*

I was angered that he dared to challenge me in the least. *I'm a human. He has no idea who he's messing with. Damn him!* Soon my thoughts switched to the lesser of two evils. *Would a tiny bite hurt that much?*

I found myself bargaining with the flying devil. *Make it quick and tiny. Not a big red mark or lump. Something little that won't itch.* "Come on! Just do it already. Please?" I pleaded into the darkness. I became confused from delusion and lack of sleep.

Knowing full well that I probably would not sleep that tonight, or any other night for that matter, nearly made me suicidal. Sure, I could have reached for the hardcore stuff like Valerian root or melatonin, but what was the point? He would just bite me to death. Delirium nearly set in until I reached with an outstretched arm to grab tightly at reality.

*It's – just – a – goddamn – mosquito! Quit being such a fuckin' baby and act like a man, dammit!* And with that, I accepted the fact that this dragon must be slain. Yes, me, the dragon slayer would come to *my* rescue and take the giant down.

Until you've lived in the dragon's lair, you have not toiled in knowing the harsh reality of befalling a mighty behemoth. I graciously accepted the grand task bestowed upon me by me.

My girlfriend would say this is dramatic. I began to

wonder. *Hmm, she's not here. Is there a conspiracy? Does she know the crazy flyer? Are they friends? Is he sleeping with...preposterous man. Snap outtuv it! He's making you crazy. Crazy I tell ya. Crazy!*

Over the years I have become intolerant of the disgusting insects that zip through the air. They are the bringers of bad tidings. One disgusts as much as the other. Now, in the moment, my fight was with the stinger in my room. He took residence in my sanctuary, my palace. He had squatter's rights and found solace in knowing that he was like Elliot Ness - untouchable.

"You'll slip up. You know it's gonna happen. You'll venture just a bit too far, just like an orgasm, past the edge of no return and then your buzz-happy ass is mine. Mine I tell ya! All mine!" With that I gave a laugh straight out of Jekyll and Hyde. *Jeez, he's making me crazy. I'm actually trying to have a conversation with him. Wait, now I'm talking to myself about...shit! Shit! Shit! Shit!*

I was in bed at ten and it was nearing one o'clock. I covered my head and began to sweat under the solitude of the sheet. *This is ridiculous!*

In the end, just like in the movies, man prevailed. It was a cat-like, unseen deathblow. I wiped the slime from my hand and reached for the light. I had won. My head sunk into the coolness of pillow and soon my body spoiled in the relaxation of victory. Just before I reached dreamland...bzzzzzz.

# PeekaBOO

David had a Roman nose accompanied by a strong chiseled square jaw. His eyes were an incredible luminous blue and attracted looks from all. He had hair that made men jealous and should have been on a model. He had the looks, but Katrina was no slouch either.

Men noticed Katrina. She had long legs that made her five foot ten inch frame stand at attention. Her perky naturally large breasts invited looks. She had full luscious lips that begged to be kissed. She had a round, but firm, butt that sashayed as she walked.

David loved her ass and would steal a feel whenever possible. He always thought it was her best feature. The two were a loving couple, and being childhood sweethearts, they had played in the same sandbox while growing up.

David had a fetish of sorts. It wasn't the type of fetish where he'd dress up in high heels and wear blush and red lipstick; however, the effect was the same. His rush made him feel sexy and got him hot.

David liked the adrenalin of lying in-wait to startle people, co-workers, friends, and especially his wife. He could get her every time. She knew he'd be hiding somewhere, but she always seemed to let her guard down. Sometimes, after a good scare, they'd end up in the sack because the endorphin rush and exhilaration got their juices flowing.

Katrina had announced she was going to take a shower and David managed to sneak upstairs unnoticed. He folded himself up, yoga style, and hid in the overly large linen closet before she was able to grab her towel. When she opened the closet and reached in for her towel, David, in slow motion, reached his hand out and with his fingertips touched hers. The hairs on her arm stood up and the feeling instantly ran to her neck and down her spine.

Katrina screamed so loud that the dog howled. She almost fell over the banister. Her heart pounded furiously and she thought she might pass out. David sat giggling behind the door.

David's mind was twisted. When he was installing ceramic tile he incorporated a circular saw, actual blood from store-bought animal liver, and even a fake, but life-like hand, into his scenario.

When his beloved wife found him, presumably passed out on the kitchen floor with blood splattered and a hand lying next to him, she ran to him and yelled his name. When she approached and kneeled next to him and looked into his face, while shaking him, he sat up and kissed her. She pulled away in anger and stomped off.

One of David's favorites happened when he announced he was cleaning up and then heading to bed early. He had filled the bathtub, placed a plastic children's play radio in the water, hit the power supply at the circuit board upstairs and quietly slipped into the tub. He had taped a cut power cord to the radio and made it look like the cord came out of the wall after shocking him.

Katrina, with other things in mind, made her way up the steps, while reaching in front of her in the darkness. She wore a silky pair of sleeping shorts. It was just enough material to cover her tight little bubble butt. The bottoms matched her sleeveless top, which showed off her body. She inched her way to the laundry room to flip the breaker to power the house. When she walked out of the laundry room, she noticed that the bathroom light was on. She felt compelled to investigate.

She slowly peeked around the open doorway, ready to join David in the bath, but suddenly the horror set in. She saw that David's head and arms were floating in the tub from apparent electrocution; one leg slung over the edge. She went to him and pulled his head from the water. He grabbed her and pulled her into the bath. After she swung her arms a few times, he gave her a deep kiss. They were both so excited that they did it right there.

*****

It was a windy Saturday night and David was out with his buddies catching a football game while Katrina was looking forward to a night alone. She sat with a good book and sipped chamomile tea. Later she took a long, hot bath and drank a few glasses of Pinot Noir while nibbling on chocolates. She appreciated the aromatic flavor of black cherry and pronounced spiciness that suggested a hint of cinnamon. The full-bodied and rich wine was pleasing to her palate, while the velvety texture made a good pairing with her Godiva.

She enjoyed the bath salts as the effervescent crystals dissolved on her naked skin. She liked to watch the sudsy bubbles disappear revealing her dark areoles. Bath time was her private time.

After her enjoyment in the tub, Katrina wrapped herself in her favorite cashmere robe and sat by the master bedroom fireplace. With the lights out, she could hear the gentle breeze of the night softly moving the branches of the large tree outside. The leaves brushed against the bedroom window. She liked watching the glowing embers as they became dark charcoal-like and eventually fell off making crackling sounds. The smell of pine permeated throughout the bedroom. She couldn't remember the last time she felt tranquility and pure relaxation of such a level.

Just as she began to doze off on the over-sized plush chair and ottoman, she heard the all too familiar double chirp of the house alarm go off; indicating that her hubby was coming through the garage door. Katrina was feeling a bit randy and wanted to greet him in an eager fashion. She slowly undid the velvety belt of her gown and gently placed one half to the side revealing the soft skin of her upper thigh. She wanted David to have his way with her that night.

The anticipation turned into longer than expected minutes. Waiting, Katrina called out to her lover. There was no response. She called again and again. Sensing that David was up to something, Katrina informed him, in blunt fashion, that she was naked and wanted to screw. She expected to hear him running to the party. Yet again, she heard nothing.

Katrina, now irritated, in that she felt he didn't want to ravage her body—she was upset at his childish antics. She aggressively and angrily tied her robe.

She grabbed something from the dresser and stomped off in the darkness of the hallway toward the staircase. When her left hand reached for the light switch at the top of the stairs, a cold feeling rushed over her like a wave. She became nervous and her right hand began to shake. She flipped the switch with her left and there the figure stood, dressed in all black.

Even with a masked face, she could recognize the chiseled jawline. Her thoughts complete, she had accepted her actions. She jumped back and fired once; a flash from the muzzle blast briefly lit the darkness. The intruder had no pulse.

*****

"I was married once, three years ago." Katrina told her date.

"Been there, done that," her date agreed with a pleasant smile.

"Yeah, you know how it is. The, uh, pulse of our marriage just seemed to stall, then stop. Just like that, the marriage was, uhhhh, well, let's just say the marriage was dead." She said, grimacing.

33

"Dispatch, this is car forty-two. Over?" Officer Smith asked, holding the walkie-talkie to his mouth.

"Forty-two, this is dispatch. Over?"

"Dispatch, please be advised that I have a disabled brown two-door Chevy, plate, Zulu, Alpha, Charlie, oner, niner, four. Please run. Repeat, please run. Zero occupants. Over."

"This is dispatch. Running plate on a disabled brown two-door Chevy. Please await information."

"Dispatch? Over?" Smith asked, impatiently.

"Car forty-two, this is dispatch. The car comes back clean." "Thank you. Show me investigating. Car forty-two out."

*****

The couple had a traditional log cabin set on the hillside of the Giant Tank Mountains. Joe and Lisa worked very hard and loved the tranquility of their mountain retreat. It was only a short two-mile hike to Gorge Lake for pristine water and great secluded fishing. Since no homes were located within miles of the couple, they had it all to themselves. They considered it their hidden oasis. Sometimes they would even skinny dip in the cool refreshing water with nary a wandering eye.

One particular trip led the pair on a hike to the highest peak of the Tank. It was supposed to be a half-day trip, as they needed to travel back to their condo in the city to prepare for the workweek. With one wrong turn and dead batteries in the GPS, the twosome didn't get back to the cabin until just before sundown. It was a bit late to travel back home, but they needed to leave the cozy cabin confines due to work the next morning.

"Do you realize that we never even snapped at each other over getting 'lost'?" Joe smiled.

"That's because I knew *I* could get us back again."

Lisa said with a raised eyebrow and a widening grin.

"Oh, I see how it is...," he said with a reaffirming smile, "hey, we really should hit the road. It's already a few hours past when we wanted to leave. Not a great idea to drive around here at dark. I'll load the car."

A few minutes later the two were on the road. The Giant Tank had unnervingly narrow roads with sheer cliff drops. The pavement was loose in spots and the tall pine trees made visibility difficult even on a full-moon night. Only compounding the difficulty was the animal life that wished to explore and become adventuresome in the depths of the darkness.

Joe zipped the silver Audi A4 in and out of the curves and was making quick time off the mountain. If he was nervous, it didn't show as he eased on and off the gas allowing the momentum of the car to work without breaking.

"Hey, do you see that up there? Slow down," Lisa said as she peered into the night along Joe's side of the road.

"Looks like a guy standing there. Should I stop?" "No-no. Keep driving. Pass him. Just leave." "But I can't just..."

Lisa interrupted immediately, "I said just go!"

"Whatda... No. We should help." And just like that Joe backed.

Joe's car window down, "Hey, you need help or somethin'?

"Yup, sure do. My car ran outta gas as a few miles back. Parked it right in the scenic overlook."

"Gas, hmm? Nearest station is at the bottom of the hill, 'bout three more miles."

Joe turned to Lisa and raised his eyebrows in a gesture she knew all too well. Joe's singular problem was that he was always *too* helpful.

Lisa was unsure and one look at the stranger told

35

the story. He stood crooked to one side. His brown jacket was filthy with soiled spots on the chest. The trim was coming unraveled and white threads peeked out. Ash marks littered the lapel and he reeked of cigarette smoke. The right pocket was hanging half off, obviously torn in a mad dash for smoky treats. She could see the dingy stains of tobacco on his teeth.

Joe had the car in park and was about to offer the man a ride, "Want a ri...WHOA!"

Suddenly and without warning, the man pulled a gun and as Joe turned his back and away, the cold steel muzzle met and rested on his left temple. Joe's eyes continued and looked upward to the man, his head as still as concrete.

Before Joe could mutter a word, Lisa leaned over, and without seeing the pistol, told the man that they were in a hurry. Noticing the barrel, a wave of stupidity crashed over her and she felt the helplessness of drowning.

"Did you *see* a car back there?" The man asked with a deep voice and thick sarcasm.

"Uh..." Is all Joe could muster.

"It was a rhetorical question, dumbass."

"Please don't shoot him," Lisa begged.

"Kill the lights and both of you get outta the car. NOW!" The couple did as they were told and quickly scurried out of the car.

"In front. Get on your knees!" Demanded the gun-wielding maniac.

"Please don't kill us," Joe pled. "Take the car. I have money in my pocket. Take it! Take it all! We won't tell. Just take it and go."

The would-be thief got close to the couple as they were on their knees. He inhaled through his nose to clear the snot and rolled it through to his mouth, swishing it around a bit before swallowing it down. He lurched toward the two, backing off, and coming at them again. Both turned their heads to opposite sides in fear and panic. The assailant was so close that Joe could see the whites of his deep-sunken dark eyes. Joe could smell him with every breath. The man wiped his runny nose with his bare hand and wiped it across his upper lip.

"Name's Carl," he said as he slowly rolled his tongue over his front teeth and made a sucking sound, while smacking his lips a few times. He then moved back just a bit, placed his free hand, thumb and index finger, at the corners of his mouth and then slid them down over his ruggedly whiskered face to his chin.

Lisa couldn't help but be put off by the horrendous stench spewing from Carl's mouth with the pronunciation of every short syllable as it rolled off his tongue. It was a cross between sour milk and sewage. She thought he hadn't brushed or ever met the opening of a mouthwash bottle.

"Thought you should know the name of the person who's gonna kill y'all. See, either way I get the car and y'alls money. For me it's a win-win thing. Get it?" The man, no longer a stranger, said with a slight Southern drawl and an awkward smile.

Joe, always quick on his feet agreed, but offered some realization too, "Carl, I see your point and you're right. Only thing is that, if, and it's only an '*if*' here, you'd get caught without killing us it'd just be stealing a car. I'd think a sentence for car theft is a ton less than double murder. Heck, you'd maybe just get probation." Joe could feel the cold sweat as it overtook his flushed face while Lisa grabbed his hand and trembled with fear.

"What's your name?" Carl asked.

Joe stared blankly into the chilly night. Carl double snapped his fingers, "Hey, cat got your tongue," while waving the dark steel weapon in his other hand.

"Uh, Joe."

"Well, *Uh,* Joe, those some good points you mentioned there. Both y'all get up and start walking that way." Carl pointed, with gun in hand, in the direction behind the car. "Three things though: One, give me the money. Two, watch out for bears. I hear they all over 'dese parts. Oh, if y'all get any ideas of tellin' anyone, I *will* find y'all. Cah- peesh, a-mee-go?"

Joe grabbed his money clip from his right pocket, removed the cash, and handed it to Carl. "Thank you, Carl."

Joe wearily walked to Lisa half expecting to hear gun blasts ring out and see his wife crumple to the ground in a dead heap. Lisa held on to Joe's arm as they began to walk. A few steps farther and they walked faster. They kept walking until they heard their car speed away. Lisa turned to look and saw the taillights disappear around the bend.

"My cell is in my left pocket." Joe said excitedly as he pulled it out.

"No. Wait a minute or two. What if he comes back?"

"Good idea."

"Did you see that guy?" She stammered. "He looked horrendous. Scraggly hair, torn clothes, he even had a gold tooth. A gold tooth!" She added loudly.

"I'm glad you got a good look. Pretty hard for me to see with that Glock in my temple."

"Hello, 9-1-1. What's your emergency?" The dispatch officer asked. "Hello! Can you hear me? Hello? Hel...," asked Joe as he walked the road attempting to get a cellular signal.

"Hello sir, 9-1-1. I can hear you. What's your emergency?"

"Uh, we've been carjacked! Some guy with a gun took our car! Just took it!" "Where are you?"

"Umm, hang on. Honey, what's the mile marker

say?" Joe asked while pointing at the metal sign along the roadside. "Okay, we're on Overpass Road in the Giant Tanks at mile marker 119."

"We have an officer in the area. Someone will be there to help you shortly. Can you describe the person who took your car?"

"Okay, wait a second. Here's my wife..."

"Hello. It was a man wearing a long-sleeved, jersey shirt." She said very fast. "Ma'am, please slow down. Just breathe." The dispatcher offered.

Lisa took a few deep breaths, "The shirt was white with blue or black sleeves. He had long scraggly hair; his jeans were ripped at the knees. He was wearing boots." Lisa was still shaken and spoke very fast, but she managed to pause enough to be understood. "That's about...Oh! Oh-oh, wait...wait! He had a gold tooth, too." She said at the last second.

"Thank you, ma'am. Just stay right there. I'll send a car to get you two."

"Car forty-two this is dispatch. Come in car forty-two." The dispatcher said into her radio.

"This is forty-two. Go ahead."

"Car forty-two we have a couple who have been carjacked. They're holding at mile marker 119 on Overpass Road in the Giant Tanks. What's your location?"

"Uh, close by. I'll swing over there and take care of it."

"Car forty-two, I show you responding. Dispatch out."

"Uh-huh. Okay. Bye."

After almost an hour, a car approached the stranded couple. At about two hundred feet, the pair could plainly see it was a police car.

"Oh my god, thanks so much for getting here!" shouted Lisa as she walked towards the officer.

The officer had a strident gait and walked towards the two while in the process of removing his hat with his head tipped slightly while his hand reached towards his head. His looks screamed military-like precision: brilliantly shined shoes, laces perfectly placed, a hard crease in his pant legs, which hit in the exact center of his shoe tops. His badge was polished to perfection proudly displaying his name: Smith.

His shirt was deep-brown, crisp, and plainly starched. Officer Smith had his equipment and weapons belt weighted down, but in perfect alignment to his uniform.

Smith had all the usual tools for his job: .40 caliber standard-issue, stun gun, ammo clips, walkie, and cell phone, which all looked in just the right order if needed in a hurry. His presence made Lisa and Joe feel safe, at least safer than they felt during the last hour.

"Sorry," said officer Smith, "but you two'll have to sit in the back. You can give a statement in the car." He added and walked to his patrol vehicle. The couple followed as the introduction pleasantries were short and vague.

"No problem. It sure beats being out here!" A happy Joe blurted while ducking into the backseat.

As Lisa went around to the passenger side, she noticed a rather full, large, black and red duffel bag sitting on the front seat of the squad car. On top of it sat a dark gray electric razor for on-the-job perfection and professionalism. A small piece of white fabric poked through the little zipper opening on the side.

"Do you want our story, um, statement, I mean?" Joe asked while trying to see through the smallish triangular openings in the metal floor-to-ceiling cage separating the front and backseat.

"Nah, we can do that at 'da station." Smith stated, his head down.

"This seems kinda out there. Do you patrol this area often?" Lisa asked as the car began to pull away into the wandering darkness.

"Nah, I'm kinda new on the job." Smith said with a quick glance in the rearview mirror toward Lisa. He cracked a light grin just enough to for Lisa to see his brief smile.

Just then, Joe felt the fingernails on Lisa's hand dig deeply into his right forearm, poking into the skin, while her hands trembled uncontrollably. He looked at her, just about to say something, but hesitated when he saw the fear strewn across her face, her eyes wide-open. He glanced forward and caught a glimpse of the shiny oddity as the reflection shined off the rearview mirror.

# Chance Encounter

The note was simple and typed in italics: *Go to the police and you both die!* The message was signed, *The Jester.*

Joe and Vicky were married for three years. The note arrived on their anniversary.

*****

Vicky Larson came from a wealthy family. Her mother, deceased, was a surgeon and her father, Ken, retired as a prominent psychologist. Dr. Ken Larson actually held a few therapy sessions with Joe. Joe came from little, but managed to get a full scholarship to Oklahoma State, where he first met Vicky. The two dated briefly in college. She went to medical school and he ventured to Europe. She landed in Kansas City for her residency; he concocted stories of intrigue and novelty.

Joe sold a few novels and was attempting to become a writer, while doing IT consulting on the side. Vicky made it through three years of hell and became a doctor. She joined a practice in the Southwest. Joe was en route to the outskirts of the same area, but neither realized it. It was fifteen years since they had parted ways.

On a warm, sunny Sunday morning Joe was sitting alone at a small grated table with a weather-beaten umbrella. Outside the downtown coffee shop, he saw a dark-haired brunette get out of her car. *Wow, she's gorgeous!* He thought as he looked over the rim of his mug.

She paused at her door momentarily, while adjusting her oversized blue and black infused sunglasses and grabbing her brown leather handbag. *Damn! Those black yoga pants make that ass pop! And that orange and yellow fitted top...dark hair...shit, looks hot!*

She turned to walk to the shop, and Joe immediately lowered his head, slightly out of embarrassment of staring, and because he feared that he may have actually mumbled his thoughts out loud. His lowered, burgundy baseball hat sheltered him from her wandering eyes. He began to tap away at his keyboard, lightly feigning interest, but keenly aware she was approaching. She passed without a thought.

Joe kept typing away that morning, but every few minutes his gaze wandered up to see if she was coming out of the shop. Wanting to take another look, and in somewhat stalkerish fashion, Joe packed up his computer and ventured inside.

*Shit! Shit, Joe, She's right there!* He made sure to keep it in his head so no one could hear. She paid for her to-go order and turned right into Joe.

"I'm so—sorry," she said politely.

"Uh...oh...that's okay," was all Joe's lips could mutter while he bent down to pick up her purse. As his hand reached out for the small black leather clutch, he noticed a photo badge hanging on the side. He stopped immediately and his heart pounded as if he'd just ran the hundred-meter sprint.

With his head slightly tilted upward to look at the woman, a smile began to cover his face, "Vicky? Vicky Larson?" He asked as he removed his cap.

"I—don't—believe—it! Joe Anderson!" And that's how Joe and Vicky became reacquainted.

*****

He casually approached the café entrance. He wore a solid dark blue baseball cap with no logo and, as instructed, with the brim pulled low. Joe's biceps bulged in his black short-sleeve t-shirt. He had on his favorite pair of grey fitness pants for comfort and ease of movement, and a beat-up pair of red and white tennis shoes.

Referring to the threatening note, Joe walked inside and veered to the left, nonchalantly. As he walked, he began to count off the booths in his head: *One, two, three...* He slowed his pace before seven, and reached into his pocket. Just opening, the café had three customers, two of whom were at the counter.

It all came into place, just like The Jester had told him. The man had his cap- covered head deep in the newspaper. He was sitting alone. The letter was written to exact specs of the layout and design of the café. A car was parked in the spot Anderson was told it would be placed. A hat ensured that the cameras would not view his face. The plan was now in action and there was no turning back.

Joe's hand shook and he feared he'd be seen. He walked past number seven without so much as a glance at the customer and went into the restroom. His hands shook visibly. His cell phone rang as he entered the toilet stall. "Mr. Anderson, what do you think you're doing?" said the man, using a voice-altering gadget. "YOU are compromising the mission!"

"Are you insane? This ain't gonna work!" snapped Joe.

"Oh, but it has to work or she dies! Now, put on your big-boy pants and finish the job!" Joe could hear a slight giggle and then The Jester abruptly ended the call.

"Shit! He's actually watching! Dammit! Dammit! Dammit! What the hell did I get into?" Joe mumbled to himself, hoping for a response of reason to talk him out of this situation.

Joe walked out of the restroom and circled the coffee stand in the center of the restaurant. He made a right turn and stood staring at booth four. Joe took a quick glance back to number one and did a fast count as he slowly stepped. *Five, six...* He reached into his pocket and pulled out a syringe. *Seven!*

The hat-wearing man in the booth had his back to Joe and was unaware of any pending danger. In an instant, Joe secured the syringe in his left hand with his fingers clasped tightly around the object. In one swoop, he jabbed the needle in the man's neck while pushing the plunger to expel the unknown whitish fluid. The stranger turned and locked eyes with Joe.

When he saw the stranger, Joe's eyes grew large like quarters and a cold sweat rolled down the sides of his face. Joe suddenly realized exactly what he had done. The unknown stranger was a stranger no longer. Mr. Anderson had just killed Mr. Ken Larson.

*****

Vicky's brother, Thomas, was an active and boisterous young man who had seen the back of a patrol car more than once before age twenty. He played the stereotypical spoiled rich kid like it was his destiny. Although his parents did not allow him to go out, he would sneak away after bedtime and join his friends in deviant behavior.

Just before his twenty-first birthday, his father, old-school in nature, gave him an ultimatum: *Shape up or ship out.* Tom chose to ship out and became estranged from the family. When Tommy turned twenty-five, he was broke, divorced, and living in a rented room above a pizzeria. He smelled like pepperoni and the neon sign kept him up most nights. He made twelve bucks an hour doing warehouse work, mostly receiving and counting packages. He hated his life, his job, and he blamed his father for everything.

*****

Thirteen years later, slouching at the second table from the front door, Thomas, watching everyone, made notes. His full beard, long hair, and hat afforded him anonymity while sitting, hatching his plan.

He was there, eating breakfast in the café noting the security system. Mentally listing every camera in his head, closing his eyes, visualizing from the front door past the booths and then to the back, side door, he counted. He went to that coffee shop everyday for two weeks...hatching his plan.

**Ambiguously Enigmatic**
You think it's this and you think it's that.
Is that a hand lying in that vat?
It could be—or could it be?
Only your mind's eye will truly see.

# Ace

It was a dry, sunny day and the springtime heat soared above a hundred and ten degrees, while thermal waves could be seen radiating off the leather-cracked and sun- dried desert floor. It hadn't rained for nearly four months and the nearest cloud was somewhere over Utah. The severe triple-digit weather took care of the weak in the harsh landscape. Ravenous hordes of ground-dwelling insects scurried every which way with their morsels of goodness after attacking decaying animal corpses.

Off in the distance, just before the foothills of Montaña Poco, Spanish for little mountain, there it was, an elongated, but unassuming hole. Stevens wasn't sure what to make of it, or how it got there, but he instinctively knew it was man-made and shovels had been used to dig it.

He investigated further. The footprints could have been from the past week, as wind would have surely sifted the dirt from place to place, covering any manageable tracks. Even the slight outline of the shovel lying on the ground at one time was left intact.

Paul Stevens hadn't been with the department for long, but he was definitely eager to make a name for himself. He felt that he was constantly living in the shadow of his father, a former detective famous for solving a rash of serial murders that had struck the small oceanside town for over ten years. With the new murders, now was his time to shine.

The first body appeared washed up in Archibald's Bay, smashed against the rocks from countless waves and a powerful current that could have ripped it in half. The remains took a week to identify. The second, a man in his mid-twenties, had been discovered under a bridge leading to Trout River. He was clothed, but his shirt was torn from an apparent struggle during his strangulation.

The third person, a lady in her thirties, had been found along a lonesome stretch of highway leading to the desert, just on the other side of the mountains and far from the first two murders. Her throat had been slit. The fourth victim had been found in a trash dumpster at the Desert Oasis Trails parking lot. Paul was on the path to finding the fifth body in the desolate barren land.

All of the victims had a crucial element tying them together: an ace of spades playing card on each corpse. Instead of being black, the spade was colored over in red. It had been done in marker. Stevens had collected four and was now looking for the fifth.

A bit of forensics digging and the figure began to appear. More sifting through bone-dry dirt showed evidence of a red shirt, blue jeans, boots, and a leather glove. Paul hesitated for a moment as not to unsettle the find; he paused further to peer near the deceased's head. Stevens bent over and cautiously picked up a small piece of thick paper lying just under the blood-crusted hair. There it was, the ace. The detective had little to go on with the playing card. Every dime store in the country sold playing cards, and these were simple to the very edge.

Even though the case was getting tense and the public demanded answers, Stevens needed a day to recharge and get his thoughts straight. In times like this, he usually went to his dad's place located just above Sheepskin Hollow. It was a traditional log cabin that overlooked the gorge, with the whitewater of the Trout River churning below.

Paul could always count on his dad for guidance and a few good stories about battling the bad guys. Paul's dad was not due back at the house until tomorrow—away on a fishing trip. Paul thought he'd get one day in by himself in the tranquility that was Sheepskin. After trekking the canyon trails and dipping a line in the river,

Paul decided to head back and throw his feet up for some R&R. He lit a fire and before long the scent of pine filled the house.

He broke out some of his dad's Rémy Martin XO Cognac. As it slowly trickled out of the circular-spoke, wheel-shaped bottle and down the side of the bulbous glass, Paul thought that a cigar might be just the right fit for the fire and nicely aged, and extravagantly distilled, brandy.

He crept into his dad's back room, sneaking as if his father might catch him at any second, and found the humidor. Paul even looked around in a sneaky manner like a teenager making sure he wasn't being watched. Without hesitation, he grabbed a thick and darkly wrapped Casa Magna Colorado Robusto, one of Nicaragua's finest. He brought it to his nose and took a long deep inhale of the intoxicating aromas and accents of the rich tobacco.

Stevens, cigar in-hand, plopped down in the leather, espresso-colored, high- backed chair and threw his legs up on the matching ottoman. As he reached for his drink, he saw a dulled black, metal box on the bottom shelf of the wooden side table labeled, "Case Notes." Always wanting to learn from his father's experiences, Paul instinctively grabbed the box and began to sift through a mound of random scatterings.

He stumbled upon some old news clippings from his father's days of detective work. One article, "Death in the Hollow," described the series of grisly murders that preceded the capture of the serial slayer known as The Ocean Killer. Many of the bodies had been found along the beach so it was assumed that the killer had a boat and dumped the bodies at sea.

There were articles in a separate file in the box. Paul rummaged through to see what the killer's M.O. was back in the early eighties. He read on, only to find that thirty years later when it came to the business of murder and mayhem, times hadn't changed as the slayer either strangled or cut his victims. Just then, Detective Stevens noticed his father had circled a sentence: "The killer left behind an ace of spades playing card with the center ace scribbled with red ink."

A cold chill ran up Paul's neck, as his first thought was that a copycat killer was on the loose. *Maybe it was the son of the original killer? Was the killer still alive and released? Was the wrong man convicted?* He quickly jotted a few notes. He scanned some of the remaining articles and comments and then came across pictures.

Paul passed through old photos of his father's war days, with a few individual medals thrown into the mix. Sergeant First Class, Thomas Stevens, was a powerful looking figure decked out in his uniform. Thomas served bravely in Vietnam and had the hardware to prove it. Paul shuffled through a few more pictures before coming upon one that caught his eye. It was a photograph of his father, sans shirt and holding an M-16 appearing quite muscular with sculpted abs and chiseled arms. A feeling of pride swept over him knowing that his dad once looked like that. Like his father, Paul had a military career that eventually launched him into police service. A few years on patrol and he passed his detective test and was a full-fledged investigator.

He sat sipping expensive alcohol and smoking a wonderfully redolent cigar in front of a roaring fire in a hand-built log cabin in the woods wondering his next strategic move in the case.

The three snifters of cognac, mixed with a dinner of grilled trout, made him sleepy. He snuffed out the fire and made sure his cigar was no longer lit and headed off to bed, eager to see his dad in the morning as his newly created notes were awaiting answers.

The next morning Paul heard shuffling about

downstairs. He rose from his slumber and grabbed a thick, black-hooded robe from the back of the door and headed down to greet his father.

"Good mornin' bright eyes," his dad greeted.

Paul threw out a big yawn, followed by a reaching stretch, "Mornin'. How long have you been here?"

"Oh, I got in about two hours ago. Went to pick up the mail about an hour ago. It's a beautiful mountain morning out there," he said, while pointing toward the open window.

"Yeah, a bit chilly though," said Paul, cinching his warming robe to keep out the draft of the mountain air.

"So, how's the case comin' along?"

"Not good! Found another body the other day. Hey, I came across some of your old notes last night..."

"Uh-huh, I saw the box opened when I got home," his father interrupted.

"Yeah, anyway, the Oceanside Killer that you captured...I read your note about the ace of spades found at the murder scenes. I've found the same cards at the five murders so far."

"And?" Thomas asked.

"And? Ya think it's a copycat? Relative? Was the guy released?" Paul asked, as his voice got louder with each question.

"Could be a copycat, but doubtful that it's a relative. The guy was shanked in prison over a debt. I read that he died on the dank, dirty floor of his cell in a pool of his own blood. When I was closing the case, I found no relatives or immediate family members. The guy was a loner."

"Shit!"

"Yeah kid, I hear ya. Sometimes you need to dig to the roots."

Paul knew exactly what his dad meant. He needed to start at the beginning of the first murder and work his way through every single dust particle of evidence.

Paul made his way to the living room and got comfy in the cozy chair near the fireplace. He noticed that his dad had removed the metal box and cleaned up from Paul's evening. Paul searched the room for the box, as he wanted to read more about the serial killings that had tormented the small town. He wanted clues. He needed answers.

"Hey, Dad, where's that black metal box from last night? It was right here." Paul stated while pointing to the dark end table.

"Oh, that old thing? I put it in the coat closet. Why? Do you need it?"

"I wanted to finish some of those articles from the Oceanside killings. Who knows, maybe sumthin'll spring a trigger in my mind and help the case," he said, walking toward the coat closet.

Thomas couldn't get a word out before Paul reached for the box on the top shelf of the closet.

"Dammit!" Paul shouted as the box top came off and the papers and other items scattered about on the shelf.

"Take it easy, wouldya. That's my life's work!" Thomas said with an defensive chuckle.

"I got it!" Paul stammered back as he nonchalantly pushed everything back into the box with one hand while standing on his tiptoes, unable to see the top of the shelf.

Paul took a seat and began to quickly read the articles. As he glanced from one article to the other, he looked up at his dad, "Oh, looks like some of the photos are still on that top shelf in the closet. They must've slid out when the lid came loose. I'll grab 'em when I put it back."

"No worries, son. I'll take care of it," Thomas said with a comforting smile.

"By the way, I saw your 'cliché' picture," using air

quotes, Paul was laughing, "ya know, the one without your shirt, flexing the guns? You're holding your M-16. Cliché dad, very cliché." Paul said, shaking his head and smiling.

"Hey, everybody was doing it." His dad laughed while muddling around in the closet.

Thomas stood on the stool so he could find the clutter of photos and clippings on the shelf. He quickly sorted things out; paper in one hand and pictures in the other. As his hands came out of the darkened closet into the light of the room, he looked down at the top photo and turned that stack upside down.

He handed the papers to his son for more reading and hopefully for insight, while he slid the photos deep into his sweater pocket. The top picture, in full color, was just as commonplace as Paul had said it was: there stood Thomas in full gear next to a hulk of a man. Scribbled on the bottom, "Good luck Ace!" the ace of spades card was proudly displayed in the front of his helmet. The card showed the spade in the middle, the center marked over in red.

# The Elevator

"That's what I said, it cut his hand clean off. The doctors had to amputate the arm at the elbow," the officer told his new captain.

"Yeah, okay. But, how'd it happen in the first place?" the captain asked.

"He charged me and all I could do was grab the machete lying on the ground. My gun was lost in the fight and the Taser wouldn't come out of the holster. It got stuck on the goddamn strap. As I jumped out 'da way I swung and lopped off his hand at the wrist with one swing. There it was, a bloody hand clutching the knife," Casper described while using his left hand, wrapping it around his right wrist and shaking the limp hand.

The two shared past war stories while fighting crime in the line of duty. Officer Casper received a call for domestic violence and took the right hand of a disagreeing and argumentative ex-husband.

"He went in for a seven-year stint, even got himself a hook for a hand," the officer said.

John Casper came from a long line of police officers. His father was once a cop, his younger brother was an officer, and his grandfather was a law enforcement specialist too. John only had six more months until he could realize the pleasure of sleeping late and doing all those odd jobs around the house. He already had his retirement date picked out: March 30th.

Casper had an extensive and exemplary career in law enforcement. He loved being on the street where things always happened. He had a need to be in the middle of the action. He fought crime for just over thirty years and looked forward to an early retirement.

It was a blustery, snowy day in early February when the call came over the radio: "We have a four fifty-nine reported at 2-1-2-2 West Anderson Lane. Respond."

Casper swiftly grabbed the two-way, handheld radio control and pressed the button, "Car twenty-two, show us responding. Over."

"Car twenty-two this is dispatch, show you responding. Over."

John disliked many things, but he couldn't stand it when people took things that weren't theirs, so taking the burglary call was top on his list. He also knew that not many burglaries went unsolved, so he had it in his mind to solve this one soon, before his retirement. He and his rookie partner rushed to the scene.

"Okay, ma'am...no ma'am...ma'am, can you please calm down for a second? We need to get a statement." Rookie Patrolman Smith asked the upset woman.

"Boot, ya need to calm her down so we can get the info. Can't get the info if she's all hysterical n' such. Get that info, boot." Casper, the wily veteran, said while laughing and shaking his head at the struggling rookie. He loved giving the headache problems to the newbies.

"Lady, you're gonna hyperventilate. Take a few deep breaths and focus," Smith suggested, while gently holding her arm and motioning her to sit on the concrete step of the wooden porch. He could hear her begin to take deep breaths in through her nose and exhale long and distinctly through her mouth. He heard the air as she blew it out. "That's better. There ya go. Let it all out."

"I came through here," she explained, pointing to attached garage entrance door near the back laundry room. "Then, there," she pointed to the long interior hallway, "he ran through there. I didn't see everything, but he had on a dark blue winter coat, dark beanie hat, and dark gloves. I thought he was wearing brown boots with yellow and brown patterned laces. You know, old school-looking type things."

"Ma'am, I need you to tell me if anything's missing," Officer Smith directed.

"Just my laptop. It was a white Mac, about this big." She motioned with her hands to the size of about a medium pizza box. "Had everything on that thing too. Ya gotta find it. You just got to," she declared.

"Of course, we'll do our best. Is there anything else?"

"No. No, I don't think so."

The officers took notes, pictures, and asked the neighbors if they saw anything out of the ordinary that day. The victim timidly went inside to clean up and rid her house of the chill and nastiness that had occurred. Once she was convinced that she had removed the bad energy from her home, she headed to the kitchen to prepare dinner for a family who would be home soon and running about. She just wanted things to be normal very soon.

She pulled red, green, and yellow bell peppers from the veggie drawer in her side- by-side refrigerator and gently set them on the orange, plastic cutting board. As if guided by instinct, she reached to her knife block for her favorite chopping knife. It was laser sharpened and guaranteed to hold an edge for fifteen years. Her hand found nothing. Distraught, she phoned Officer Casper to have the knife added to the list of stolen items.

*****

The thirtieth of March came faster than John realized. He never solved the burglary case and now it was up to his young mentee to take over and find justice for the woman and her family. John knew Smith was up to the task and even asked for a phone call once it was solved.

Three days later, however, ex-Officer Casper was back at the precinct, heading to payroll on a different floor. He needed to update his new address in order to receive all of his pension benefits. It was his first time in the front lobby "Civilians Only" elevator in nearly twenty years. He always used the one in the back of the building labeled "Law Enforcement Personnel Use Only."

John was on his phone and didn't pay much attention to anyone on the ride from the ground to the floors above. As the elevator cleared and passengers scurried onto the fourth floor, the recently retired John Casper stood against the back wall waiting patiently to regain his cellular service and finish the conversation with his wife.

"What floor?" The man in the winter jacket standing at the elevator control panel asked.

Casper, heading to the eighth floor to human resources, looked the man up-and- down and, feeling extremely bare without his police belt, got his cellular signal back, "Honey, I'll call you later," he said to his wife after watching the man remove his winter gloves and seeing that he had no right hand.

Whitney Sanders sat on the cement stoop of her father's old, now dilapidated ranch-style home and waited. It was where she grew up. It was where she hid her scars. She noticed the cracked concrete on the step, just near her feet, and her eyes followed the randomness as it spread into various veins near the edge. She reached down, and with her perfectly manicured, clear-coated fingernail, delicately flicked a tiny chipped flake from the crack and watched at it as it descended onto the sidewalk below.

"Hey, he got off. The jury rendered their verdict a few hours ago," she told the man on the other end of the phone, while her other hand rummaged through her fashionably elegant Burberry tote bag until she saw the silvery flash of metal. She gently removed the item from her purse and gently placed it on the step, covering it with her leather handbag.

"Are you okay?" he asked, concerned for her psyche and wellbeing.

"Uh, I'm——uh——good. I'm okay, I guess. No..." she momentarily hesitated, "no, it's good. Uh...I'm just worried for my little sisters," she told Manning through the dull reception on her cell phone, as she sat, patiently waiting in her sleeveless, snug, cotton v-neck, summer dress. It matched perfectly with her subtlety sexy, shiny black ankle-strap sandals.

It was an unseasonably, downright hot and muggy, pants-sticking-to-your-legs day in the early fall of 1991 when the little girl went for her first day to Whitman Middle School. She started sixth grade, and at ten-years old, little Whitney Sanders was blossoming into a young lady. She was ahead of other children her age, and even ahead of the older kids in her grade in mathematics, reading, language, and science. She was a bright child and she wanted to become the first female President, or a neurosurgeon like her father.

By the time Whitney was well into her second year at Stanford, her mother had left her father due to the drinking. The once skilled brain surgeon had taken to the bottle like metal to a magnet. He said it relieved the stress of having to save people, literally having their blood on his hands, and being the one who had the power to make people better. Somewhere in all that self-loathing, he failed to notice that he had become an alcoholic.

Her dad got remarried near the end of her third and final year in her undergrad. His wife was about to have twins; two baby girls would be added to the family. This was the same time that Whitney decided to attend law school instead of medical school. She went to Stanford and graduated at the top of her class at an age when most students were just entering the school of law. She made partner by twenty-six and eight months later she opted to leave the firm and start on her own. By the time she reached thirty-years old, she had the most successful practice in Nevada.

It was around this time that her father ran into other problems. He was arrested for molesting a child in Andrew's Town Park. The victim said she was touched while playing on and crossing the monkey bars. The little girl told her mom, who, in-turn called the police. In the official report it was written that Mr. Sanders inappropriately touched the child while 'helping' her off the apparatus.

Now grown up, unmarried, and just over the initial phase of having started her own law firm outside of Las Vegas, Ms. Whitney Sanders sat in the darkness of the warm summer night and watched as a fluttering moth tempted its fate and tested its guile with the heat of a flickering incandescent bulb near the black light pole in her father's front yard. She noticed how the pole sat on an odd tilt and deduced that the contention in her dad's life was similar to that of the old, rickety fixture.

She contemplated what she might say to her father when she saw him. *Hi dad. It's been a while.* Those were the only words she could imagine saying to the crotchety old man. Just as her desire to leave kicked in, she saw the low, dim lights of a car turning down Johnson's Creek Drive. The driver of the large, rectangular sedan slowed, stalled briefly, and then parked the vehicle behind Whitney's jet black Cadillac CTS.

It was a long fall from his days of practicing life-saving surgery. Having to resort to low-level consulting jobs was a far cry from the exceptionally high-paying, six-figure income he had received from his striving medical practice. Gone were the luxurious cars, the metallic green speedboat, the wild and extravagant parties, the indulgence, and the self-applauding respect. And, from the look of his once opulent house, the financial means for restoration and remodel disappeared from the coffers too.

As her father walked from the exceptionally narrow, blacktop street to the walkway to his home, it all came back to her. Suddenly she was that little girl back in 1991 getting ready for her first day of middle school. She saw it in full, vivid color as if it was happening in front of her in high-definition. A tear rolled down her cheek as the memory rushed back. She felt a twitch, and then an uncontrollable shake took hold of her.

She watched as the man meandered side-to-side, one foot next to, and then over the other, and weaved his way up the path toward her. He wore a chevron-style mustache, thick and wide as it covered his entire upper lip. It grayed near the corners and mingled with the wiry, coarse browns.

He had just been acquitted and celebrated the only way he knew how, by finding the bottom of a full bottle of whiskey.

"Hi, hu--n--ey!" he said in a long, drawn-out, slurred speech while pointing his index finger in the air for a strange type of non-essential emphasis. He sported a sheepish, awkward smile to accompany his alcoholic stupor. She looked at him, flabbergasted, with her eyes wide open and shaking her head. A rush came over her and her mind raced to her two, innocent little sisters.

"Honey? HONEY! I haven't seen you in...I don't even remember how many years, and you have the gall to call me *honey*. You god-damn-bastard!" She said angrily, with serene detachment, extending and rolling the words into one to express her feelings.

Whitney took one hand and ran her fingers over the drawcord closure; rolled leather handles, and polished metal hardware of her exquisite purse. While it was large enough to carry a small infant, Whitney never really carried much.

Underneath her exquisite satchel, Whitney's tiny right hand securely, but loosely, held onto the black, synthetic polyurethane grip of a thirty-eight special handgun. It was a snub-nosed, short-barreled weapon with a small-shrouded hammer designed for easy cocking. Again, she thought of her little sisters.

# The Closet

Jeff didn't go into that closet. It wasn't *his* closet. He didn't even step near it. As far as he was concerned, it was a closet full of what-the-hell and whatever. It was none of his business.

There were times when he imagined that his girlfriend Cindy had it filled with expensive purses, belts, and fine high-heeled Italian leather shoes. Other times he'd picture it loaded from wall-to-wall with top designer gowns and formal wear so full it took two hands *and* arms to create space for new garments. Once he imagined it was chock-full of sexy lingerie. Hell, he even pictured it complete with sex toys and dominatrix outfits. All he did know, however, is that it was the *only* closet in the house with a lock and it was off-limits to his prying eyes, but not his wandering imagination.

Jeff would sometimes write wild stories about the only locked closet in the house. Since Cindy was a neat-freak, Jeff penned a bizarre story of how that closet was her one spot to let loose with her secretive junky and clutterbug ways. *It was laden with unlabeled boxes of all shapes and sizes, mismatched shoes, broken jewelry, and socks without partners,* he wrote. *In the far corner, leftover Christmas ribbon and an unopened gift box. The top shelf, lined with purses from the '80s. One corner hid a pair of genuine clogs circa 1979. In the jewelry pile was an original Swatch Watch - the one with a blue and red band with yellow face - sans battery. It was a disheveled mess at best, but cleverly locked away,* he finished.

He had no idea what that closet meant to Cindy. It was more than her place to hide all that was old in the world of fashion. It was a ceremonial place. It was her comfort. It was her therapy.

On a cold, lazy Sunday, with the aroma of burning

cinnamon scented candles filling her house, Cindy's eyes slowly lifted over the rim of her sage-colored mug of Earl Grey Lavender tea. "Darlin' how about we get outta here for a few days next weekend?" she said between sips while looking at her future husband.

Jeff loved it when she spoke in her cutsie Southern twang. He could never resist it. He didn't care that she used it to her advantage with her cute slang as the words ran through his head. *Hun'. Y'all gonna come over tanight? Can y'all air-up my tires? I'm fixin' to come over. I all got a hankerin' for you tanight.* In her he knew he'd found the perfect partner: faithful, honest, trusting, and full of integrity. She was knock-dead gorgeous too, and that didn't bother Jeff in the least.

He was a bit puzzled why or how she'd be able to get away on short notice. Being a high-profile surgeon, Cindy had patients, partners, files, and that damn cell phone - all of which required her attention. Three days before the weekend, Cindy got called at midnight to a medical emergency. Jeff, now awake, decided to meander through the house - her house.

He strolled downstairs for a glass of water. He walked past that damn closet, looked at the doorknob, and kept walking. He stopped mid step, shook his head as if to say, *uh, no,* turned and walked back to the door. His right hand slowly reached out and his fingers gently grasped the knob. He couldn't resist the attraction. Jeff took a deep breath and turned the knob counter-clockwise. Expecting nothing, Jeff was startled when the knob disengaged the door. "Holy shit, it's unlocked," he whispered in the darkness of the night as if someone might actually hear him.

Hesitant, and a bit nervous, but curious and persistent, Jeff softly pushed the door open while his pulse quickened. Jeff took another deep breath and felt for the switch on the wall and turned on the light. There it was, in all its stunning glory...an ordinary very plain closet. Laughing and shaking his head, Jeff wasn't sure why the secrecy or fuss over such a vanilla closet.

Somewhat amused at the "revelation," Jeff took a quick glance and turned to close the door. Suddenly, he felt a coolness coming from behind him. He went back into the closet to find the breeze that chilled his neck. *Is that A/C? Is there a fan in here?*

Jeff stood in the middle of the closet and scanned. His scan developed into a peering. Behind the hanging dresses, near the corner of colorfully hung belts, and cleverly tucked behind what Jeff found to be a movable shelf of expertly arranged purses was a sliver of light coming from the wall. He set his cool, sweating drink down on the wooden shelf.

It was now about 12:30 in the morning and Jeff wasn't certain when his honey would return, but that closet, that light, the fact that Cindy was gone – Jeff pressed on and peeked through the tiny door into the looming light. He saw nothing. Nada. Zip. Zilch!

*Well, that was a huge disappointment,* as he let out a big sigh. *What the hell's with this damn door anyway? I gotta check it out.* A keen urge to find something, *anything*, Jeff moved the purse shelf and opened the tiny door. He lowered his large frame and crawled through the low-ceilinged, narrow space for about twenty feet.

It was a different world. Not like that of "The Lion, The Witch, and The Wardrobe," but it had Jeff a bit freaked out. Dim lights, a massage table, plastic all over, drab-white walls, and a very cold presence made goosebumps rise on Jeff's muscular arms. Once his eyes adapted to the dimness, he saw what appeared to be droplets of crimson in a small curved line. *Whoa! In a room with a hint of pine-scented cleaner, that deep color seems to come from nowhere.*

Suddenly on the tablish bed, a closer look brought

into sight a sheet with tiny slash cuts and finely shredded material. Maybe his eyes were playing tricks on him, but Jeff's mind swore he saw the silvery flash of metal in the pure white light in the room just smaller than a single-car garage.

Jeff, now wide-eyed, slowly turned his head to the adjacent wall where he noticed what he believed to be chains complete with wrist cuffs and locks. His eyes penetrated past the chains to notice a large wheel board. *What the hell! How'd I miss this stuff?*

He wanted to turn and run, but his feet felt like they were stuck in a deep, thick mud. He drew a blank, lost stare. He was certain that he should not proceed. He took a seat on the plush, brown couch in the corner. It only happened to be a quick seat as Jeff heard the muffled sound of the garage door opening off in the distance. His mind now fully engaged, his body reacted accordingly and he turned and bolted to bed.

Cindy tiredly meandered up the stairs. When her left foot landed at the top step, her head turned to look towards the closet, but it was so much work that her eyes lazily shifted down the hallway and her head followed suit. Though she hesitated, her right foot met the hallway landing and she slowly walked towards the master bedroom while undressing. Her clothes strewn about and completely naked, she opened the linen closet and grabbed her cashmere blanket to keep warm.

She ambled into the bedroom and felt a draft come over her as if a window or door was ajar. Unflustered, she wrapped the comforting blanket over her body and snuggled in next to her Jeff to sleep.

Jeff, feigning grogginess, slowly lifted his head and faintly opened his eyes and with a low sleepy moan, "Hi honey. You're back. I missed you." Cindy draped her arm over her honey and she could feel his heart beating fast. He kissed his sweetie and both drifted off to sleep.

Cindy saw everything in her Jeff that she never saw in other men. He was a gentleman. He understood her quirks. He wanted to be with her and *only* her. She would often sit and recall the jokes that made her laugh. She knew from his laughter that he appreciated and liked her silly side. She could tell that his easiness actually calmed type 'A' personality. She knew through his actions that he respected her. She loved him, but above all, and most important, she knew he loved her for her.

Cindy disliked liars, cheats, and her personal space being violated in a manner that was obtrusive and disgusting. At fifteen she had been stopped on the street and asked if she'd be interested in money for sexual favors. She ran home. That's the very first glimpse Cindy had into the mind of horny men. It sickened her. At twenty-five, and in medical school, she had been grabbed and forcibly kissed in front of her boyfriend. Another glimpse. At thirty, engaged doctor after married doctor after married doctor constantly asked her out. It was another filthier glimpse of men wanting her.

Along with the physical groping, she felt psychologically raped by men. Sure, it was just a delicate shoulder rub while she was sitting in the doctor's lounge, but did he really need to press his hard-on into her back too? Fed up and about to crack, she needed a release so she agreed to go out to dinner with a married doctor to teach him a lesson about values.

*I know I shouldn't be doing this, but I feel alive, electrified. He can't stop me. I'm a strong, confident, unflappable, unstoppable woman. I'm smart. I'm a frickin' surgeon! He'll see. I should...nah, I'm in control, while feeling uncontrollable. That's it! No one will control me.* Cindy had the thoughts all day before her date.

The very married Doc Gentry picked Cindy up at seven sharp. He tried to kiss her at her door; however, she boldly withstood his advance. "Naw Gent, that's no way to be a gent," she said with a giggle and a bit of her Southern charm.

The night progressed and drink after drink Gentry felt more reassured that he'd be doing Cindy later that night. He checked quick lists in his head: *She's laughing at my jokes. Check. She's making eye contact. Check. She's occasionally touching my arm. Check. I think she rubbed her foot on my leg! Check and Check!* Then in a moment of sheer bravado, Gentry placed his right hand on Cindy's knee and slowly slid it upward. He was anxious to see how far he'd get. He wanted to bang her right there.

"Gentry! What kinda lady do y'all think I am?" Cindy announced as she removed his advancing hand from her thigh.

*Damn it!* Gentry muttered inside.

"Maybe another glass of wine? I know the Merlot here is a great vintage!" He managed to muster after his dismal attempt.

"Well, sugar, if y'all say it's good, it's gotta be down right excellent then. Sure thing, I'll have a glass, but only the one. I have to drive and at my size, two glasses is plenn-ty."

Gentry deviously ordered an entire bottle because he had other plans – he wanted to do the driving - to his house or hers. To him, it really didn't matter. Just after the wine arrived, Gentry excused himself to the restroom. While he was gone Cindy sent a text to her Jeff, who was at his house watching football with the guys.

Jeff thought that his little Cindy was at a work dinner meeting. She hated that she didn't give Jeff the truth, but then again, he never asked. "Hey sweetie, I'm still at this boring thing. How's your night going honey bun?" Her next text shot out just as quick, "Gonna be a late one. Talk to ya tomorrow. Smooches darlin'." Jeff, reading her messages, simply responded, "All is well. Game is good. We're winning! Chat tomorrow, sweetie."

Cindy dropped a pin-sized amount of Rohypnol mixed with half a 100mg dose of crushed Viagra in Gentry's glass. A few quick spins of the bulbous stemware and no one was any the wiser.

Gentry slowly sauntered towards the table, being very careful to allow Cindy to notice him. He slid in and sat closer to Cindy than he was all night. He nonchalantly adjusted his platinum Rolex and made sure to lay his wrist in plain sight.

Cindy realized she might need to play along a bit in order to get her man. Gent tried one more time and placed his hand on her thigh. Cindy was unfazed, but allowed his hand to remain in place. The Super Viagra that Gentry had popped while in the restroom began to kick in and his pants were jumping. He had yet to take a sip of wine. His hand began to move on Cindy's thigh. He'd been envisioning her naked body all night. He wanted her.

"Naw, sugar, you ain't takin' a single sip of that wine. It's so yummy. Look, I've gone and drank mine all up." She said in a tipsy, teasing tone. Gentry slid closer.

"Cindy, I think you are simply gorgeous. I've wanted you for so long I can't stand it! I see you strolling in the hospital, alone in the lounge, walking to your car; alone, always alone." He moved his hand up her inner thigh and she did nothing. The doc looked around as if he was going to make a confession. With no one in earshot, he leaned in, "I want you. Now!" His hand slid further. "I popped the blue pill earlier. Let's go!" he said with a gentlemanly smirk.

"Finish your wine and then, then we'll go." Cindy said with a quick wink.

Without hesitation, and in unfashionable wine-drinking custom, Gentry downed his Merlot in three massive gulps. Cindy still in full tease mode, slowly moistened her full, red-stained, velvety lips and softly asked, "Just what is it y'all want to do with me, hun?" She smiled, slid away, and got up from the crescent, leathery-lined booth.

Cindy walked towards her car and Gentry followed closely. His hand reached for her butt, but she was just a bit too quick and he missed. Five steps from the car, he insisted on stopping.

"Come on naw. It's right there sugar. And I'm right here! Have a seat and you'll feel much better darlin'," she said while opening her passenger door for the stumbling Gentry.

He plopped his butt in the car and oddly began to use his hands to lift his legs like they were full of lead. Each foot dropped to the car floor with a thud. He had lost control of his legs.

Cindy sped home, less than five minutes away. She could see that Gentry was almost ready and pulled her car right into the garage. Gentry reached for the door, but Cindy was already at the passenger's side letting him out.

"Come on big fella. Let's go!" Gentry had plans with her, but little did he realize Cindy had thoughts going through her head as well, very unexpected thoughts.

Doc Gentry grabbed at his lips like he had just received a numbing shot to his mouth. "Can yoooou hwear mwe?" Mwe. Mwe? My wips fweel fwunny," he mumbled as he stumbled with Cindy's help. "Hey, my wegs dwon't werk!" Cindy leaned him in a corner near the inside door. She raced over to the water softener and reached behind it. Suddenly a shelving unit moved to the side and a door came into view. She grabbed Gentry and helped him through the door.

Inside, Cindy hit the light switch and Gentry saw starbursts and blurry images, waves of black ran past his eyes, but he had enough faculties to notice what he thought was a bed. "Is 'dis where we're gwonna do it bwaby? My wips still fweel fwunny. Gweez, I mwust bwe dwunk! Twake me!" he shouted as he stumbled and fell onto the stationary table, pants falling down.

Cindy quickly undressed, grabbed her tyvek and then added a blue woven bouffant style, polypropylene head net and got to work. All of her devices were playfully arranged in order of size, from biggest to smallest on the cold, shiny tray. With all the Viagra, removing Gentry's black, pure silk boxer briefs was the most difficult part of his upcoming transformation. Cindy's mind went back to what brought her to this point of no return.

It was in the Big Box store where a vagrant had assaulted her. The police officer friend, with whom she felt protected, had tried to have his way with her. The geeky, very married doctor who kept asking her out to dinner. The ever-present..."I'm married, but getting a divorce," South American tour guide who forced his way on her on the dance floor in a foreign country. She could *feel* his revolting presence, his stares, the touches, and the innuendo with his rapist eyes.

Dr. Cindy Mendel wanted to circumcise the demons from her past. She felt that killing her self-appointed guilt would allow her the repose she desperately desired. She would watch as the shallowness and defiance slowly left a quivering body and felt the anger and rage flee her own presence.

The good doctor finished her work, cleaned up and discarded her carnal remains, then entered her house through the garage doorway. She dropped her leather, raspberry- colored purse on the chair of her mahogany dining chair. The supple bag landed on the cushion with a thud. She climbed the staircase, exhausted and drained. She pressed her right hand around and grabbed the oak railing tightly to pull her up the steps.

71

When she reached the top hallway, she didn't have the energy, but opened her closet door anyway. She walked through the oversized doorway, flipped the light switch, fumbled with a few things on the chest-high shelf and turned to walk out. She fell into her pillowy-soft bed and quickly drifted off to sleep.

"How was your day, honey?" Jeff asked after a sip of his full-bodied Cabernet.

"Fast. It went very fast. It was nice. Glad it's finally Friday. It was a loooooooong week," she said between small bites of her puttanesca.

"Hey, all we need to do after dinner is throw a few things in a carry-on and then take off tomorrow for the bed-and-breakfast. Maybe a glass of wine at home? We might even have time to mess around before bed," he said with a big grin.

The two shared a slightly chilled bottle of Pinot while nonchalantly tossing a few clothes in the black travel bag. Cindy needed to add one small item before zipping the bag closed so she playfully marched down the long hallway to her closet. Cindy opened the door and remembered that she had left the light on from the night before. Unfazed she went to her purse shelf, stood on her tiptoes and reached for the small black clutch. She patiently worked it to the edge until it fell into her hand. She bobbled it twice, but it eventually made its way to the floor.

As she bent down to grab the purse, her gaze stopped upon a circular water stain on the third shelf. She couldn't recall ever bringing a glass into her closet, let alone setting one on her very expensive, solid cedar shelving. Thinking it was strange; she played it off as being too busy and not remembering. Jeff was already in bed, sans clothes, and ready for some fooling around.

"Awe, not tonight, hun. I'm so dead tired. How 'bout we save it for tomarraw, darlin'," she said in her sleepiest twang. While lying in bed, it dawned on Cindy that, not only did she not have a glass of anything in her closet, she'd never taken a glass in there, ever.

"Whereya goin'?" Jeff mumbled, sleepily.

"Bathroom."

"Mmmm," he groaned, turning onto his other side, away from her.

Cindy, walking down the hallway to the other bathroom, stopped. Thinking about her past few days she hesitantly sauntered to her closet. Turning the knob, entering, closing the door behind her, she examined the shelves.

*Hmmm. Interesting. Water stain—not mine. This purse was moved. Don't remember using it in forever.* She shifted a few larger bags and then knelt to the floor. "Well, that explains things," she muttered, reaching for a piece of broken clear tape. *Hmm, looks like Jeff's been busy in my closet. My – fucking – closet! Mine!* Getting up, closing the door, she lazily walked back down the hallway.

Sitting on her toilet, contemplating, Cindy knew what she wanted to do. Changing her want to a need, she found her way back to bed.

She looked at her one and only that morning while he lay with a lifeless peacefulness, still and motionless next to her.

## The Great Outdoors

Waterfalls, trees, and grasses surround.
Streams to cross over with a single bound.
A car horn toots the annoying noise.
You hit the gas and lose all poise.

# Two Inches

The two had a few bumps in their ten-year marriage. There were the usual things that separate people in love: lies, deceit, resentment, disdain, and eventually lack of trust because of the appearance of a mysterious phone number.

Amy had visited every state except Alaska and Tony wanted to surprise her with a trip to her last one. He secretly planned everything, right down to the Pinot Grigio they would share during their shore lunch of fresh salmon with lemon sauce and sweet white onions, poached red skin potatoes with rosemary, and wild asparagus grilled to perfection with the spears just a little browned during the chartered fishing daytrip. It turned out to be the trip that would be remembered for a lifetime.

He had emailed the guide way ahead of the trip to find a beach that, during low tide, would allow the couple to harvest razor clams. The extremely tasty delicacies were unique to the Kenai area and were cherished Pacific seafood. Tony wanted to be certain that it would be a perfect and romantic lunch.

The couple worked hard on their bond. He knew things about his wife that she had never told him, she didn't have to tell him, but he knew. He knew of her lies, but pushed it off as just being her way. He always found out anyway, but usually much later and well after the fact. He played it to her upbringing and having to keep things from her prying parents. It was her perpetual habit.

"Howdy! Name's Eli, but you can call me Buck. Everyone calls me Buck. You can call me Buck too." The fishing guide explained to the couple in a smoking-induced, raspy voice.

"Hey, Buck! What's the plan for today?" Tony asked.

"Well, we's gonna just motor on out 'dat way," he pointed to the North, "and uh, then probably float for a wee bit and drop a few lines. Then we'all will boat on up toward the Peninsula, grab a bite of shore lunch, and head back. Should be a grand day!" he added with excitement.

"That sounds like an adventure!" Amy said hesitatingly as she was unfamiliar with *real* fishing.

"Hey, it's really not that big a deal. It's not like we're fishing for Jaws or something. They're about this big," he said as he stretched his arms about two-feet apart. "You'll do great." He added for encouragement.

The only fish Amy ever caught were with her little cousin at the local fair in the kid's trout pond. It was cane pole fishing at its finest.

The group set out into the pristine and flowing current of the churning river. The sky, dark in some areas, gray in others, but blue and inviting in the direction their boat headed. It showed to be a clear day.

"Naw, ma'am, like this," Buck said as he showed her how to wrap and snap the security cord on her orange life vest. "Yeah, there ya go." He added as she made proper correction.

*****

It should have never happened the way it did, but once Buck had that massive coronary, everything went haywire. While trying to revive their guide, the boat spun out of control. Completely unprepared, they entered the rapids and bounced around in the whirlpool of riptides and fast currents until the hull of the bow ripped apart on a jagged underwater boulder. The sharp, torn metal hole was the size of a basketball and the front of the boat filled with water more quickly than either of them could handle.

It took only a few minutes for the eighteen-foot, welded aluminum river runner to capsize with the black and silver fifty-horse power Mercury outboard motor upside down, only showing the stainless steel prop blades. The couple stayed with the boat, bobbing up and down in the swift moving water. Their bright orange lifejackets kept them afloat while they clung to the vessel.

"We need to make a break for the shore!" Tony yelled in between spitting river water from his mouth. "There, aim for there!" He pointed to a boulder along the shore, just past a calm tide pool.

The couple began to swim together, but the current pulled them apart. Amy made it to the boulder, but Tony ended up farther down stream on a little beach area lightly covered with water-polished creek pebbles. Tony knew that, during the drifting and sinking of the boat, the two ended up off any regularly navigated water channels. With darkness looming he also knew that they needed to get a fire going very quickly.

They stayed close together and collected any bits of dry wood they could find. Grizzly bears roamed the rough and rugged terrain and often wandered along the river's edge. Tony was ready for everything and the fully stuffed, waterproof backpack he took on the fishing trip was just another example of his preparedness. He had a few energy bars, a black polymer and carbon safety flashlight complete with serrated edge, a classic fourteen-tool and six-blade, red Swiss Army knife, and most importantly, dry safety camping matches.

The two got the fire started, and for safety and warmth, made it as large as possible. "Mrs. Wilkes, may I interest you in a delectable pistachio and chocolate chip, granola-filled energy bar?" Tony asked with a smile, trying to add levity to their situation. The two took turns grabbing little nibbles from the bar and sharing some of their only bottled water, while warming their hands and drying their clothes near the roaring fire.

With the crackling logs and bright orange embers in the background, Tony offered life to the gravity of their situation. "It's Saturday night, so the river is closed to guided trips tomorrow and Mondays are closed to fishing. We are pretty far of the beaten path to be seen. I think we need to hike upstream, and hopefully we can see some boats tomorrow. If we don't find anything, we may need to prepare for a longer stay."

"We almost died back there," Amy pointed down stream for emphasis, "and you're so damn calm. The guide is dead and floating - somewhere - out there. *DEAD!*" Amy yelled in between crying convulsively.

Tony stepped next to her, held her comfortably with a warm hug, and kissed her softly on the cheek. "Honey, you've been very strong. I'm scared too, but I know we need to be composed or we'll be screwed. I need you to be tough. Let's do it *together.*"

"Okay," she said while shivering from the brisk air. The two tried to get some sleep during the long night.

"Ah, it's a beautiful, brisk, but gorgeous Sunday morning and we made it through the night with no bears visiting camp," Tony said, stretching his arms.

"What's next, upstream?" Amy used the universal hitchhiking sign with her thumb pointing behind her and over her right shoulder.

"Yup, but that way," he said while smiling and pointing in the other direction. The two grabbed the little gear they had and headed along the bank.

After only a few feet, Tony stopped mid-step, hesitated, and cautiously looked over his left shoulder to see a large gray wolf standing just atop the deep cut edge of the riverbed. He gently grabbed Amy's arm to alert her of the animal.

"Stare right at it. Don't let it think you're afraid. Face it," he whispered to his trembling wife.

The gray, with head lowered, but eyes up and nostrils flaring to sniff the air, just stared at the couple. Amy quickly had an image of her St. Bernard in her head and noted how much bigger the wolf looked than her dog. The thought only made her shake more. The animal took two long and skillful leaps into the wooded area and was gone.

"What the hell!" Amy shouted, unnerved.

"Could be a sentry. Could be an omega." He said calmly, while eagerly peering into the trees. "The sentry will decide if we're able to be conquered, so to speak. The omega could just be a lone wolf kinda thing."

"Uh, WHAT? How do you know?" Amy asked franticly.

"Discovery Channel." He told her without missing a beat and still leering into the pines. "We need to keep moving - now." Tony added, knowing that either way, one wolf or a pack would be back.

They traveled aggressively along the water's edge as the spray kicked up the dirt. The two, bedraggled and out of breath from the rugged haul waited nearly three before a rest.

Amy - exhausted and her feet hurting - plopped on a rock and removed her life vest. She had a distant look in her eyes, and it wasn't one of looking for wild animals on the hunt. It was a look that Tony saw too often lately.

"Hey," she said unenthusiastically. "I have to tell you something..." Tony interrupted her.

"Does it have to do with *that* look you have and have had for the past few weeks?"

She hesitated for a moment, looked at the stones, and slightly pursed her lips on an angle, "I guess. There's no easy way to say it, but..." Tony interrupted her.

"Then don't. Whatever it is, it can wait. Make it the first thing you tell me when were outta this mess. How's that sound? It'll be what we talk about over a nice dinner near a warm fire." He said with a smile that told her whatever it was it really didn't matter, not now, now later, maybe not ever. The wilds of Alaska, like a doleful and contentious marriage, are a lost and untamed frontier.

"Uh, okay. Deal!" she said as Tony slowly turned his head away.

"Sonofabitch!" He yelled while staring down the creature that had tracked them during their three-hour trek. It stood about ten yards away, parallel to the river, but just far enough for an easy escape. Amy turned, in disbelief, to follow Tony's pointing finger.

"Shit! Now what?"

"We move - fast!" he said, with the first hint of worry in his voice.

As the couple negotiated the landscape along the creek edge, stumbling over large rocks and around immovable boulders, Tony kept an eye on the tree line for a possible surprise hunting party. He still had the brief conversation in his head of his wife's attempt at something. *A confession.* He thought, but quickly discarded it from his head.

His focus was on survival and getting to safety. Tony and Amy were in a fast- paced walk, side-by-side, and occasionally bumped into one another from the stumbling on and over large river rocks. It was difficult for Tony to hear with the wind. His backpack made a swooshing from the nylon material rubbing along his floatation vest.

Ahead the crystal-clear, glacier-filled stream rushed faster and roared viciously. Out of the corner of his eye, Tony saw the slow trot of several long silvery-looking legs swiftly weaving through the poplars and black cottonwood, with eyes on their quarry.

"We need to cross!" He yelled to be heard over the rushing water and steered Amy closer to the edge. They could hear the deep sound of their heavy, wet shoes sloshing in the water. They were in the moment and completely aware of their surroundings, but the water had different ideas as the two traversed the frigid glacial flow.

The current was waist-deep and moving downstream was tremendously difficult. Tony had a firm and safe grasp on Amy's arm. He wasn't under control of his legs, but rather guided them as the gushing undercurrent pushed them forward without his effort. He felt his shin bounce off the jagged rock formation and then his foot caught another and he went under while letting go of Amy's arm.

Amy went sideways after slipping on a moss-covered rock. Tony, back up, grabbed for her, but she was swept away by the current. She bounced off rocks like a pinball, barely able to keep her head above the water. She was churned about in a crucible of torment until she finally clung to a log wedged between two large shore-side boulders. Tony, life vest intact, floated in a half swimming, half bobbing manner.

Amy saw her husband quickly floating in her direction, but her hold slowly slipped from the drenched, soft wood of the branch. Tony closed to mere feet when Amy got pulled from her clenches by a fast swirling current. All he could do was follow her down the stream.

He kept his focus on her body, which was moving violently through the thundering whitewash. He could barely see her arms flailing just above the water. Suddenly he saw her go under. "Amy! A-M-Y!" He yelled while his arm reached out in front of him to nothing. As fast as she went under, her head reappeared above the surface and he saw her tossed around in the wash like a rag doll.

Tony swam frantically to get to his wife, but the distance seemed insurmountable and the water kept him from her. He slipped into a swift current and that one flow kept pushing him towards her. He looked up to see her hands grasping at a fallen pine tree crossing the creek.

When he finally got to her, she was under the water and her fingernails were digging into the decaying, waterlogged wood. The swift current directed Tony to the shore and he quickly pulled himself out and up to his feet and began to sprint the short distance to Amy.

He could see her hands, well above the water, flailing about in search of help and rescue. He ran while keeping his eyes fixated on her. He never saw her head above the water when his running jump landed him very near her submerged body. He could stand with his head well above the surface, but Amy was lodged between two huge jagged rocks in the center and deepest part of the river.

He could feel her arms and he slid his hands up under her shoulders. He pulled, but her wriggling body didn't budge. He tried again, but nothing. He took a deep breath and went under the swirling water to breathe life into his wife. She gasped, uncertain what he was doing. He came back up for a deep breath and then went under again.

He breathed into his wife's mouth to fill her lungs with air. Once again, he popped above the waterline to recapture his composure. He tugged and tugged on his wife's body, but the rocks would not give her up. It was as though their death grip only tightened.

She was only a few inches from survival, as he saw the life drain from her wide- open eyes. He clung to the tree while looking at her body undulating in the flow under the water. "I knew. I already knew." He meekly said into the cold, crisp air. He knew. He saw the hidden, flirtatious emails, the sexually provocative texts, and even the secret hand gestures at the last block party; he knew all too well.

As he reached to feel her pale face and close her eyes, "I cheated too," he somberly muttered.

Tony raised his head and turned his gaze to the end of the fallen tree, but the unfiltered rays of the reflective sun created a flash in his vision. In his peripheral sight, near the sprawled roots, he could make out the majestic image of the gray beast slowly stalking and walking towards him, one large paw in front of the other with a snarl that showed the oversized canines and razor sharp incisors.

# Natural Selection

Jerry sloshed through Coast Rican jungle terrain and hacked at overgrown branches with his rusty machete while occasionally stopping to swat off the attacking mosquitoes coming at him from all directions. Trooping in full-netted 'squito gear, as he lovingly referred to it, only kept the flying torpedoes at bay for a short time. One always worked its way under the layer of no-see-um netting to explore Jerry's tender, juicy, blood-laden skin. Their dining was delectable as Jerry was a fair-skinned, white boy with a fear of the dastardly beasts. Fear made the blood sweeter for squeeters.

If it wasn't mosquitoes, it was Charles "Charlie" Alexander the scientist whom Jerry had to fend off. Jerry had past challenges with Charlie and he considered the man a pompous PhD and who wasn't afraid to let everyone know it. Charlie's main target was always fat little Jerry.

Charlie was a swarthy, dark-eyed man with Bond-like looks. He didn't fit the prototypical scientist mode; a model maybe, scientist no. It was Jerry's assertion that Charlie used defensive characteristics and tactics to project his true feelings of insecurity onto others. Jerry just got caught in the way.

It was on the third day of exploration that Jerry discovered a wiggly, squirmy creature and dubbed it the squigglywig because it looked like an earwig, but had squiggly-wiggly characteristics.

As Jerry observed his new found bug, he noted the carmine color, the tentacles on its side, and the alarming rate at which it grew. He found that the longer it got, the more it took on its surroundings. It was as if the creature attempted to blend in and camouflage with the leaves and scenery when it felt too large to hide. Jerry decided that a dissection must take place to truly understand this new find.

Jerry was alarmed to find that after making the bisection, the insect worked its way back to one piece. Another cut, back together again. Jerry watched in amazement at *his* discovery. He decided to take a break and placed the squigglywig in a small, covered terrarium.

Jerry's squigglywig not only had the ability to reconnect after bisection or dissection; its legs got longer with spiky prongs at the ends. The skin became tough and leather-like. The head became three times the size of the circumference of the body. The thing had a lizardly appearance and moved in short bursts and then held still in a frozen or statuesque state.

Jerry noticed its most alarming quality, it would split in two when being attacked. This confused the assailant and the head and important parts got away alive. Even more astonishing, the headless body generated a new head if not caught. The parts regenerated almost overnight as if nothing had happened at all. The insect appeared not only bigger and faster after the regrowth, but stronger too.

He wished he could harness the amazing find and recreate it in people, beginning with himself. *This shit is better than steroids and more powerful than HGH!* he thought. Jerry decided he must share the news with his fellow entomological peers who were interested in identifying new creatures and life forms.

"Dr. Glendale, this is truly fascinating! If we could develop these properties of regeneration in humans, we could, perhaps, cure certain birth defects, abnormalities, and limb loss. It'd be a miracle before our eyes! Most interestingly awesome science!"

Richard Glendale was the only physician asked to attend the trip. Dr. Richard

Glendale III, MD, was a robust, but gentle man. He tried to find the positive in Jerry's discovery. He could see the sheer enthusiasm strewn across his face and tried to meet it with focus and education.

"I'm sure this type of happening in humans could aid in curing an allotment of problems; however, harnessing the true power and vitality of this find may prove difficult at best, Jerry," Doctor Glendale stated. "We must remain optimistic; however, it's only 1987 and surely science will be onto these developments within the next few years," he added.

Jerry had thoughts of immediate wealth. Sure, he would help people too, but the money would surely flow. The paparazzi would follow him snapping pictures and flashing bulbs. He'd love it. He'd do all the big talk shows, and maybe Oprah too. A book deal would soon follow his fortune and success.

Wanting to desperately disprove Richard, Jerry removed the terrarium from the subject tent for more research. In his shelter, Jerry watched as the squig wriggled about, over and around the branches and leaves. It moved swiftly, but stopped frequently to survey its surroundings. Suddenly Jerry noticed that his squigglywig had somehow managed to either reproduce or regenerate so there were now two wigs in the tank. Truly fascinated, Jerry realized the potential of this rare finding. Tired, he drifted off to sleep, using *War and Peace* as a pillow.

The jungle temperature dropped that night and Jerry's new find had already reproduced while in captivity. A baby squigglywig found its way through a minute crack between the warped top and the ridge of the glass enclosure. It slid its way to the sleeping heap of warmth on the tent floor. The newborn worked its way up under Jerry 's wool blanket and into his boxers. The ultra-tiny creature then wriggled back-and-forth until it was comfy cozy inside Jerry's penis. From there, down and inside Jerry's body it went. Jerry, discoverer of the unique, woke bright and early the next day, none the wiser, and feeling great.

Jerry, against the advice of local guides, went out alone for an early morning trek. He decided that he wouldn't wander too far, opting for a simple path close to the base camp. Jerry enjoyed the colors of the jungle, a sight he rarely found time to take pleasure in while tromping for science. Without noticing and before he realized, Jerry was well off the trail and deep in the rainforest. He had no idea where he was or how to get back. He walked farther.

The next step Jerry took proved to be fateful. Out of nowhere, he felt a sudden searing pain in his ankle and a pressure that made his entire leg swell. Jerry looked down to see that his limb was caught in a poacher's leopard snare. The stinging and throbbing were so intense, causing a temporary numbness, while the teeth of the snare dug into Jerry's tender flesh. Blood oozed out. When his daze lifted, he could hear the metal fangs scratch against his bone. The pain took Jerry from various states of consciousness; in- and-out, in-and-out, the hours turned into days.

Jerry realized he had but one decision: amputate his leg. He realized that it had been a long time since he had been lost. He had little water left and had run out of food about two days back. Every thought ran through his mind. *Where the hell is the damn poacher? Shouldn't he be checking his snares regularly? Should I cut below the knee or above the ankle? Why hasn't anyone found me? Where are they? Is anyone even looking? Fuck!* He was certain they were searching for him, but just couldn't find him in the intensely thick undergrowth.

He began to nervously chew on his fingernails, one after the other until he satisfied his carnal fear with aversion. Jerry used his sweaty, stinky black bandana as a tourniquet, which he tied tightly midway up his calf. He had no sensation in his lower leg, ankle, or foot. He decided that he'd use the machete to lop off the ankle. He envisioned a mighty swat and the ankle lying in the trap; however, he knew the dull serrated blade would not separate the ankle in one fell swoop. Timid at first, Jerry worked up the courage and his will to survive took over.

Through the skin, the nerves caused the most excruciating pain, and then to the bone, Jerry slowly pulled the blade back-and-forth with precision making sure to add more pressure with every stroke. Jerry's hand was holding so tightly to the machete that his fingers began to turn purple. He wanted to let go, but he was only partway through the bone. He couldn't stop, not now. Deeper and deeper the edge cut. Finally, there, on the moist jungle floor laid Jerry's right foot. Droplets of blood fell upon it, but for the most part, the bandana was doing its job.

By the time he crawled and hobbled back to camp, it was a little over a week since his disappearance. Jerry took residence in the medical tent and was given a steady diet of IV fluid.

In Jerry 's absence, Charles, PhD, had taken it upon himself to examine Jerry's squigglywig.

"I agree, Richard. There's an upside to fully researching this *thing*." Jerry could overhear Charles telling Dr. Glendale as the two were just outside the med tent.

"Well, Chuck, this *thing* as you refer to it is Jerry's find. Perhaps he has notes and logs already in place. We should ask..."

"Jerry? Jerry got lost taking a piss and came back minus an ankle! Jerry? Really?" laughed Charles as he walked off.

Jerry's ordeal in the lonely jungle had lasted for nine days. He had spent two days in triage. On day thirteen, things started to happen.

\*\*\*\*\*

For some reason Jerry was a definitive host. The squigglywig didn't lay larvae; however it could regenerate within Jerry's body. Jerry's leg began to grow at an alarming rate and within five days he had a fully functioning ankle and foot.

"For chrissakes, Jerry! You're foot. You're fuckin' foot!" Charles shouted while pointing to Jerry's newly grown limb.

"I know. It's amazing! Feels just like the last one too." Jerry added with laughter and a smile.

"If this could happen to Jerry in the middle of a godforsaken rainforest," Dr. Glendale said as he spread his arms wide open, "the possibilities for the rest of the world, with proper medical care, could be, well, endless."

The discovery group entered their last week and changes in Jerry kept coming. One morning, during stand-around coffee and granola, while stories flew and the treetops ruffled, almost instinctively, Jerry dove to the ground at the sight of maggots moving on the leaves. He never balked at the taste of the white wiggly things. He scrounged for more. He suddenly developed a maggot pica. Alarm swept throughout the group. Jerry decided it was time for him to rest and he grabbed a seat just past a large jungle fern and near an anthill.

Jerry, ready to relax, knew something was about to happen. He could feel it through his foot, to his ankle, all the way up his leg. Then, there it was. He could feel a tentacle slowly penetrate his abdomen. The pain was deadening, but the rush of adrenalin shot to his heart making him feel powerful and conquering. He was ready.

He decided days ago that he wanted to take the journey to the other side. This would be *his* time. He would be the leader. That's the only reason he'd do it, to lead *his* troops. He'd be the Dr. Charles Alexander, Pompous Jackass PhD to the squigs. He'd rule supreme.

In Jerry, the eggs were laid and he was quickly morphing.

Suddenly Jerry was snapped from his thoughts of almighty dictatorship and world supremacy with a thunderous groan from the jungle depths. Trees shook and a bellow proceeded to blow a foul stench from within. He'd never heard anything like it or smelled something so gut-wrenchingly awful.

Jerry's toey tentacles quivered. He could feel the push of vomit extruding from his now swollen belly. Acid hit his throat, followed by bile and blood. The taste made it all worse and expel much faster. In a projectile vomit of force and velocity, Jerry's large intestine flew out – all five feet if it. The eggs needed room and began to take over.

"Jerry," the voice spoke in a full baritone, "You're a bitch. You've always been a bitch, but now you're *the* bitch." A deep disturbing laughter followed. Jerry could hear rustling, but saw nothing. His insides burned and he felt faint.

He crawled and pushed his way to a giant Kapok tree for comfort and security. He gently rested his head on a thick vine wrapping the base of the massive trunk. He dug his remaining toes into the cool dirt to relax. He reached out for a Red-eyed Tree Frog and chomped it in one gulp.

He momentarily felt at peace. Then like the changing wind, Jerry was overcome with an eerie uneasiness of complete disbelief as he felt his rectum pucker tight like it was vacuum suctioning the jungle floor. Suddenly, and without warning, Jerry's posterior began to convulse. He was giving birth.

One-after-one, ten squigglywig hatchlings scooted out of Jerry. He *was* the bitch yet again. Moving around quickly, they all crawled on Jerry and began to suckle from him until he was ever so slowly drained of his blood. Still alive from instant blood- revival and regeneration, Jerry was reduced to an onlooker while his followers fed.

As mother Jerry attentively watched his busy horde of squigglywigs scurry about in search of prey, he couldn't help but remember a quote by the German philosopher, Nietzsche, "All great things bring about their own destruction through an act of self- overcoming." How soulfully true that seemed now as his throng of minions ravaged the likes of the working group that Jerry had come to know as friends. He listened painfully and watched in horror as deep dark moans turned to silence, as bit by bit every piece of flesh and bone was devoured and absorbed. The wigs transformed into squiggly giants of destruction and a ravenous horde of flesh eaters.

Dr. Alexander, while his sharp, pointed tentacles were in the midst of retracting, took a massive scoop of Jerry's tissue and plopped it in a plastic bag. With his eyes still a bit protruded, Charlie let out a sigh and a shook his head, "You poor pathetic bastard! There goes your self-led dystopian future. Now people will thrive in a healthy, regenerative society thanks to *me*."

Charles convulsed and his head twitched uncontrollably. His left leg shook as if he was tapping out the beat to a top ten hit. His right arm occasionally jumped as if entering a myoclonic jerk, just like before falling asleep.

*****

Ten years later Dr. Charles Alexander developed Jerry's Link. No one knew, but the special link was Jerry's DNA. Yes, a little bit of Jerry was in every new body part clinically grown. Jerry made it from Pacific Slope to Petrie dish to functioning limb. "Thanks to good 'ol Jer, folks can be fixed up after losing that leg...uh, or ankle" the great Alexander thought loudly while cracking a smile.

*****

91

The website read: *The leader in regrowth, regeneration, and natural limb development. Dr. Alexander is the world's leading specialist in DNA Link Creation (DLC).* The information went on to state how the doctor came across his DLC find and advanced it through science and medicine.

"Hello. Welcome to DLC Clinic. Please fill out this paperwork," she said as she shuffled a clipboard full of white papers to the new patient. "Oh, I'll need to see your insurance card and ID too," the lady behind the greeting desk added.

"Yeah-yeah, no problem," the man said while digging into his pants pocket for his cards. "Is Dr. Alexander running on-time today?"

She leaned in and whispered, while looking at a chart, "He's about twenty minutes behind right now, but it shouldn't be too long," she added a smile to make the man feel at ease. "And, just to remind you, please put your last name first and your first name last on the top of all forms. People always miss that little part."

"Okay, got it." He said as he walked toward an open chair.

The man moved in the open room, squirmed into his seat, and began to write at the top of the first page, LAST NAME:...

The patient never got a chance to begin filling out the forms before the nurse made the announcement.

"Jerry Tankmeyer." the nurse shouted from the slightly open door into the room. Jerry sauntered to, and then followed her down the long hallway.

"Please have a seat in here. The Doctor will be in shortly."

Jerry sat with his head down, thinking of the past, his time in the jungle, the ridicule, and the humiliation. The door slowly opened as Doctor Alexander walked in without looking at the patients intake form.

92

"Hi. I'm Dr. Alexander." He said while turning away to close the door.

Jerry raised his head exceptionally slowly and stood. "Hello, Doctor."

A reddish, dirty-brown, pin-point tentacle protruded from Jerry's index finger while he held it close to his leg. Doctor Alexander's eyes grew large as he recognized Jerry's face under the years of change.

# The Fallen Hike

It began with a growl or roar, then the bark, a slip, an excruciating tumble, and the sighting of a Phantom Cat, which looked incredibly like a black panther. His mind told him that panthers weren't indigenous to the area. His body screamed to him that the fall left him with a terrible ache in his ankle. His face was twisted in pain as he reached for courage to move on.

Charles "Chuck" Smith always trekked with his dog, Zeus. Chuck hiked thousands of miles all over the world and over the past seven years Zeus was by his side. Zeus was a mix of American bulldog and pitbull, and Chuck found him wandering while on a hike in Colorado. The two became inseparable.

Both were on day two of a nine-day hike through the Kepler Mountains in New Zealand when the fall occurred. Chuck swore to himself that he saw the elusive Phantom cat; however, even legends said that the shadow cat no longer strolled the mountainous areas of the country. The *sighting* caused a misstep, a rock shifted, and Chuck fell about thirty feet, tumbling about on rocks and tree roots. His jolted body came to an abrupt thud against the large base of an evergreen tree.

With agility and quickness in his four-legged descent, Zeus was soon at the feet of his hiking partner ready to help. Chuck tried to shake the dizziness from his head and made an ill-fated attempt to stand. He leaned on the tree and stood up only to fall down just as fast. His ankle was in extreme pain. He could barely bear down on his foot. He sat for a bit allowing the reality of his situation to settle-in.

Chuck transferred as many of the items in his pack to the dog backpack for Zeus to carry. Zeus was strong and could easily carry one third, maybe even more, of his weight for extended periods of time. Chuck knew this would prove beneficial in his now limited physical condition.

He grabbed a thick, sturdy tree limb, and quickly fashioned a walking stick from the pine branch. A cut here and a crack against a rock there and the stick almost looked like a perfect cane. He felt rested, hungry, but rested. He decided to give it a go and the two were off.

The more he walked, the better his ankle felt. He surmised that it just needed to be loosened up. He knew better than to get a false sense of feeling better and needed to protect the ankle. He also knew the possible dangers ahead. It would be dark soon so Chuck needed a spot to drape his sleeping tarp and set out his bivy sack. He gathered as much wood as he could scrounge for a fire.

Once the flames took hold, the two settled into their cozy confines and had a quick meal: granola for Chuck and one cup of dry food for Zeus. A bit of water and it was off to bed.

The next morning brought a world of pain in Chuck's ankle. He stood the best he could and after packing up camp, Chuck hobbled away with Zeus closely following.

Limping near the edge of a hill and with rain in sight, Chuck scanned and contemplated a path down the ridge. "I'll go first, you follow," he told his four-legged friend.

He carefully placed his cane-stick and his feet followed. His stick slid on the hard dirt and in an instant, he catapulted outward and was momentarily airborne. He landed face and belly down on the ground, but on his right arm, and then slid headfirst about twenty feet with dirt and rocks ripping his clothes apart. Torn, tattered, and more injured than before, Chuck mustered all his strength to get on all fours.

After this fall, and on his knees, he offered a truce

with his surroundings and the elements; however, the lady of nature had different thoughts and a thunderous downpour created a path of slippery trouble. His tumble broke his pack and all his belongings dispersed and scattered on the hillside. He reached into Zeus' pack to find an energy bar, a pre-measured pack of dog food, and a soft pack of nothing-important-that-would-help- him-anyway.

The rain poured down and the wind blew harder and Chuck ran through the Survival Rule of Three's: "Three minutes without air, three days without water, three weeks without food, and in his situation, three hours without shelter." He said as he counted from one to three with his fingers.

He looked down at Zeus, huddled next to him, patted his head, smiled and said in a soothing voice, "Yup, we might be fucked buddy!"

Cloud cover swiftly moved in as the rain ceased and the temperature dropped. He estimated that he was still above fifteen hundred meters from the valley below. Chuck removed his now useless backpack and fashioned in into a sling for his right arm to ease the pain in his shoulder and elbow. He cut the adjustable material bindings and rearranged both into support straps, which he wrapped around many sticks to skeleton a useful pack. The smooth side of his backpack was now a rest for his forearm. His right side, from his shoulder to his ankle, was in immense and excruciating pain.

The two pushed on, Chuck limping and wincing with every step and slide of his leg and Zeus with tongue and tail wagging. Chuck made a tough decision and concluded that he may need Zeus more than Zeus needed him; he decided to ration the little bit of food for Zeus.

Chuck hiked and crawled his way down from a line just below the clouds, scratching and clawing every bit of the way; his fingernails torn and jagged from pulling his body upright from each collapse. His hands, filled with cuts and scrapes from absorbing fall after fall, were dry and cracked and began to sting. He did all of this through the jagged terrain of the fjord and over the ridge; however, he felt as though the land only scoffed at him.

"Seriously! What the hell? What else? Snow? Quicksand? Dragons? What—the—hell is next?" He yelled to the tops of the trees and beyond and then looked at Zeus, "It's okay, boy. I didn't mean to yell." He offered a soothing pat to the side of his dog.

The two hiked for several hours, taking rest stops along the way. The trail twisted and turned in the remote area, leading up and down, and over rock formations weather- beaten by thousands of years of abuse. They came to a bend and that's when it appeared to Chuck.

In his way was, perhaps, one last obstacle, a sheer fifteen-foot drop just to get to the start of the trail leading to the valley. Beyond that, he could barely see a roaring stream.

Behind him was a waterfall that was nearly two hundred meters tall with water cascading down. He could feel the cool moisture in the air as it stuck to his skin. The rocks, smoothed out over hundreds of years of constant pounding by free-flowing water, only displayed the relentlessness of his surroundings and offered no peace to Chuck. The two drank form the cool mountain water.

After little thought, but much anticipation, Chuck sat and slid over the edge of the causeway, hoping to land softly on one leg. That didn't happen as his hiking pant leg snagged the jagged corner of the rock face. This sent him into a roll instead of his hoped for gentle slide. An acute and instant pain and an intense burning sensation developed in his right arm. Chuck's hand went limp, and he wriggled and rocked back and forth on the ground in agony.

Zeus, eager to come to his masters' aid, debated

like a dog does on the high leap. Zeus slowly struggled to extend his front legs as far as he could down the flat stoney wall structure while keeping his butt back for balance. Then, in one swift motion, Zeus allowed his front paws to run down the wall while his back ones followed. This shortened his jump and he safely made it in a running motion. The dog, with tail wagging and unknowing of his partners' perils, happily gave his master a lick on the face.

Damaged, broken, starving, and on the verge of giving up, Chuck crawled and dragged his body to the mountain stream. At the bank he could feel the icy, rushing water. On the other side and just through a valley field he could see his salvation, a hunting cabin inviting him to safety.

The current was fast and swirling. The crystal clearness was inviting, but Chuck knew that it was freezing and deadly. He could see rocks just waiting to smash his bruised body, while the gushing rapids only wait for the slightest slip. He knew he had to cross.

He called his trusty companion, "Here's the deal, buddy. We need to cross this and you're gonna pull me. Or, at least make it safer."

He grabbed ahold of the pack on Zeus' back and commanded the powerful canine into the water. Mighty leg kick and thrust after thrust, Zeus was halfway across the stream when Chuck's head went under the frigid water. As if divine intervention, the pack strap tangled around Chuck's hand and strengthened his grasp.

Zeus pulled his herculean body onto the rocky bank while painfully dragging his owner behind. Gasping for air, both shook their heads. Chuck was shivering, bleeding, and unable to stand. His mind drifted for a second as he contemplated the peacefulness of drifting off.

"HEY!" he said as he was snapped out of his

loathing solitude by a huge sloppy tongue-slobbering lick to his face from Zeus. He gave his dog a hug and used his hand to squeegee off the water from his coat.

He thought about the moniker given him in college, Chuckles, and how he hated it with a passion. He wouldn't mind getting out of this situation and being called that once again. In fact, he now longed to be called Chuckles or Chucky or any damn thing anyone wanted to call him. Just as long as *someone* was calling him, anything was fine for him. He broke a brief smile and thought that somehow he'd endure and take it just as he had this trip.

His mind raced as he went through a checklist of what had occurred. He had survived the cold nights and warm days in the very same clothes that he had from day one. He had lost his food on day three of his nine-day trip, which evolved into a twelve- day survival adventure. He had eaten nuts and bugs and even sampled dog food to fight his hunger pangs. He had pulled himself over and down mountains, through pastures, and even across a pristine and freezing cold stream. He could see the cabin and it wasn't far at all.

He gathered his composure and grabbed two long thick sticks stranded by the previously flooded waters. He used Zeus' backpack to bind the sticks into a sturdy peg for stability and walking reinforcement.

Chuck, upright and hurting, began his quest of mere meters through high field grass as it waved in the wind. He limped, hunched over like he had severe osteoporosis. He used the two hip-height, thick sticks twined together, as walking crutches as he made his way through the head-tall, wind-swept grass.

The flowing breeze was strong and made his sun-beaten eyes water. He saw a man off in the far distance standing near or in a tree. It was too hard to tell with his blurred vision. Chuck made a feeble gesture with his arm, his voice was so hoarse that yelling was painful and impossible.

"Kinda wish you were like Lassie right now, buddy." He said to Zeus and only got a head tilt in return.

Chuck decided that his only chance to be seen was to make a move that his body would hate. He motioned to Zeus to come closer to his side and placed his good arm on the rear quarter of his sturdy companion for support. He carefully balanced on one leg and made a big waving motion with both arms while feeling the draining sensation of pain, mixed with frustration, humiliation, and anxiety.

Suddenly, without any warning, the biggest elk he had ever seen stood upwind in front of him. The magnificent animal was so close that he could see its nostrils flare, as it got ready to dash away. The elk never heard him through the whooshing gusts and scratchy sounds of the long grass. Now, with its immense trophy rack, it was staring him down from twenty feet, but ready to run. The man by the tree turned.

Charles Smith heard a loud echoing crack like a branch being broken by the forceful wind in quiet woods. He was in so much pain from his shattered leg and broken arm that he barely noticed the stinging sensation in his chest. Blood began to seep through his ripped, mud covered, sweat-filled shirt. The bullet went clean through the elk.

# Off My Ass

Driving down the road on a warm Sunday afternoon, Joel could see the small mountain range popping up in the distance. Having hiked the mountainous elevations, he respected the magnitude of even the smaller climbs. He appreciated the mighty view of the cloud formations clinging close to the rocky peaks looking as though they were stationary and stuck to the summit portions of the jutting tips. It was a picturesque sight with the sun just above, and in the background, while the overcast sky threw slow moving shadows with crepuscular rays producing dramatic effects. He stole a few extra looks while sitting at the intersection and waiting for the light to change.

Joel Kincaid was proud of his shiny new SUV. It had become his place of tranquility. He enjoyed the little gadgets and features. He appreciated the safety of a Bluetooth speaker for his phone.

Joel liked how the memory seats adjusted to his weight and the mirrors readjusted from when after his wife would drive the vehicle. The radio stations even had a brand- new hi-tech, advanced feature that reset and synced to his favorite stations when he drove. It was simply an amazing vehicle and he felt relaxed and at ease behind the wheel. The large twenty-four inch, deep-grooved tires gripped the pavement with improved and increased maneuverability.

Right before the left-turn arrow changed from red to green, Joel heard the toot-- toot of a car horn from behind informing him to go; however, Joel was turning right and proceeded to wait for the proper signal since securely planted on the roadside, a white rectangular sign with the words, NO TURN ON RED, written in black bold letters. Joel watched the northbound cars turn to head west, paused, checked traffic, looked at the light and began to make his right turn onto the forty-mile-per-hour road. It wasn't an overly busy thoroughfare on a weekend, but it was crowded enough for the time of day.

Joel's eyes searched down the road and in his mirrors, more for safety and out of habit for other vehicles, people, or debris in the way. He noticed that the same car from the intersection was following him very closely. The driver maneuvered his shiny red Infiniti out of one lane and into another and popped in front of the big Cadillac, just seemingly missing Joel's front end. In the traffic, the little car had only so much room before he would have tapped the car directly in front of him.

The car zipped past Joel's large sport utility vehicle and sped down the road. Twenty seconds later, however, Joel found himself next to the speedy little car at a traffic light. Joel could see the man impatiently tapping his steering wheel and staring at the adjacent signal, watching for the colors to change.

Joe couldn't help but be agitated by the person next to him, as his fidgetiness annoyed him. He decided to ignore him. The light turned green; however, with four cars in front of him, the red-car driver had no place to go. He could only wait. Both lanes moved at equal speeds, but the restless driver desperately wanted to pass to the front of the line. He switched to which he perceived as the faster of the two and was directly behind Joel's Escalade. He was so close that Joel couldn't see the man's bumper. He could only see the portion of the hood nearest the windshield and then the man's baseball-hat covered head.

Joel noticed a raring hand gesture and then another lane change and soon the Infiniti was about to pass the black SUV. Looking down the road, as he was apt to do, Joel could see a slow moving blue and white pick-up truck in the neighboring lane. The red vehicle sped up just enough to get past Joel and then tuck-in, and on the tailgate of the auto in front.

Suddenly Joel was finding his Sunday drive to the local hardware store increasingly stressful and daunting. In his mind, what was to be a drive-in-the-park-on-a-beautiful day was quickly becoming a lay-back-and-save-his-life-driving adventure. Joel decided to pacify the eagerly aggressive man by staying at a safe distance. He decided to travel in the adjoining lane and turned on his signal to indicate a lane change.

As Murphy's Law would have it, Mr. Red Infiniti and his lane began to slow down just as Joel's path sped up and, once again, Joel found himself in front of the two- door sports coupe. In his peripheral vision, Joel could see the blue brim of the man's cap as the driver turned to look at the passing ute. Soon, after a zig and a zag, the speedy sportster was just behind Joel's truck and looking to pass at the first instant.

In a split-second, and in a slow-motion, Joel watched as the car behind him got closer, as if to draft off his slipstream, pulled out in racecar fashion, and sped ahead, weaving recklessly down the road. Joel could feel the anxiety hit him as his left hand gripped tightly on the tackified leather steering wheel, while his right hand began to squeeze the shifter knob and his nails dug into the stitching along the black roan sphere. *What a fuckin' asshole! He's gonna kill someone!*

Joel saw the traffic lights ahead and watched as the green changed to yellow. He could see that the red speedster was not about to stop as the amber held for a few seconds and then turned to a vibrant red glow. The Infiniti reached the intersection, never slowed, and barreled through the changing light, unwilling to pay attention to other cars. Joel's SUV slowly rolled and then came to a stop at the front of the crossing road, where he waited for his green. His gaze went down the white, dash lined roadway where he saw the all-too-familiar sight of

Mr. Unwilling-to-Respect-Others-on-the-Road.

To this point, Joel drove the big V8-liter turbo-charged engine like it was a tiny, thin-veined 4-cylinder because he wanted to be safe and never let the powerful behemoth get away from him. He peered, about three hundred yards, to see the other driver waiting to make a left turn into a grocery store parking lot. He knew there was a short turn lane, just narrow of the westbound lane.

Joel felt a surge rip through him and a flash that took him to his days of baptism- under-fire in the perpetually dry, fiercely hellish conditions of the scorching sand and dust of Earth called the deserts of Iraq. He could feel it overtake him as it coursed through his veins, and he allowed his senses to dull, while fully engaged. In the two-mile stretch he got cutoff three times and tailgated by the same driver. Like anyone else, he could only take so much.

The light, Joel's light, flipped to green and it was *his* time. He hammered the accelerator and all the horsepower in his powerful motor responded in just. He watched as his speedometer rose and climbed quickly to thirty, then to forty, then over fifty miles per hour. He purposely steered his fast-paced missile on that fine line of concrete where the median curb met the street asphalt. He could feel his two driver-side tires running in the groove and making a rumbling sound alerting him he was wandering too far left. He ignored and kept aiming his vehicle toward the trunk of its bright red target.

He could see the waiting motorist of the tiny car looking in his rearview mirror. Joel saw that the driver's eyes were large, as he knew, and could plainly see the big black SUV train approaching faster. The previous tailgater was looking for an out, but oncoming traffic persisted and he was powerless to get away.

The former speed demon made a determination that taking a darting chance to cross the road beat being folded like an accordion from trunk to hood. He stomped the gas pedal and his fast car catapulted forward, directly into oncoming traffic. Joel slowed and kept his 'ute in a straight line and in his proper lane, watching as the Infiniti was sent spinning hit after thunderous hit. Joel could see glass and metal fly from the smashed wreck.

With a sinister grin on his face, he glanced in his side mirror to see the carnage and turned at the intersection. He immediately pulled into the corner gas station and called 9-1-1 to report the accident. Looking the short distance, he could see the Infiniti driver crumpled over the wheel, his hat nowhere to be seen. Joel watched as, one-after- one, the police arrived.

"Hey, I saw what happened." Joel yelled to the officer as he was writing notes of the scene.

"And you are...?"

"Hi Officer, I'm Joel Kincaid. I was driving west on McAllister from Andrews," Joel pointed east down the road, behind the cop, "and the driver of the red car was weaving in n' outta traffic the whole way at a high rate of speed. Seemed very impatient and just in a hurry even."

"Okay. Is there anything else?"

"Yeah, I mean, he obviously wasn't wanting to wait to cross traffic so he just sped up and took a chance. Then, there's what happened. It's extremely selfish if ya ask me; risking all those lives for what, to get a gallon of milk quicker?" Joel said as he shook his head in disgust.

"Thank you, Mr. Kincaid. Please give your information to the officer over there," the short-sleeved uniformed policeman pointed to the female cop standing in the parking lot, "and we'll be in touch if we need anything else."

After he was done with his statement, Kincaid walked back to the comfortable interior surroundings of his Cadillac, turned on the Bose ten-speaker surround sound system, firmly situated his large frame into the suppleness of leather-trimmed seat and took a deep, relaxing breath. He slowly pressed the pedal to move his Escalade forward and past the road-closing wreck. He drove close to the accident and slowed to get a better, but not-too-interested, view. He spotted who he was looking for and offered a slight head nod to the man sitting in an inverted position on the ambulance gurney.

### Stranger Things *Will* Happen

Alone at night, watching, digging my hole.
The car sped away with the life it stole.
Riding on back, it was quiet as could be.
Running for the door, I was finally free.

# No Competition

"Gonna be a hot one 'gain tonight," exclaimed Detective Larson.

"Yup, 'nother hot one," Detective Gamble added as he readjusted his belt.

"Sure hope that psycho doesn't strike 'gain. That's startin' to upset the town folk," Larson squabbled while thumbing through paperwork.

"Yup, sure is. People gettin' a bit frazzled by the murders for sure."

"Uh-huh. Ya know, everythin' we're lookin' at leads to more than one killer." Larson concluded as he threw the file on Gamble's desk.

"Two?" "For sure!"

*****

George Tate was a simple man, a rube to most, who knew very little about many things. Born and bread in Mudflap, Louisiana, he toiled away day-after-day. One thing he knew was hard work. He worked every night, except weekends. George was a loner, but he had an occasional date or two every now and then. No one stayed in George's life too long. He was a dim bulb of sorts and had a knack for, well, nothing. He had a large appetite for many things and his dreams were even bigger.

It was a muggy summer night, the kind that makes sweat bead on the forehead and gives dampness to the arms. George could feel the balls of moisture rolling down his back into his waistband. He was out strolling in the park, as stars filled the night sky, and came upon Arthur.

*****

Arthur had wrinkly weather-beaten skin. He looked as though he was baked from sun-tanning his entire life. He had tobacco-stained piss-colored teeth and his breath could have peeled paint. His big round bug eyes showed tiny compared to his wart-laden enormous hooknose. He had ear hair longer than most head hair. He wore a light grey and blue striped wool newsboy hat to cover his straggly, long black hair.

Arthur had very big, white feet with long fat toes that were disproportionately large for his tiny body. As a troll, Arthur stood about three-feet tall. He told George, with a laugh that could make dogs howl, that he was from Alaska by way of Great Britain.

"George, good chap, I've come to Mudflap to live in peace and escape the dreaded blustery days of the North. I'm done freezing my arse in the cold," explained Arthur.

George, still a bit taken aback and shell-shocked of being in the presence of a troll, just nodded dumbly, but approvingly. While Arthur gave George the creeps, George was drawn to him. Perhaps George saw a carnival act in his future that would bring in thousands of dollars? Maybe he pictured Arthur on the cover of National Geographic as the next species of human being? Maybe, just maybe, George saw a strange attractiveness in Arthur that was missing in George's life?

"You a British troll?" George couldn't believe it had he not seen it with his own eyes.

The days turned into weeks and the weeks into months. George would meet Arthur in the park after dark and the two would talk about everything. On a particular meeting, Arthur finally felt comfortable enough to divulge a secret to George.

"Bloke, I miss certain things from way back home, like black puddin', busty barmaids, and good tastin' candy floss. George, I got me a sweet tooth!"

"Yum, black pudding sounds good!"

"It's blood sausage, George," Arthur said with a chuckle and a smile.

"Sounds downright nasty! I wouldn't ever be fixin' to eat 'dat," George remarked while sticking out his tongue imitating a gag reflex.

"Ya know George, I've only been seen by a few people during my days. I never felt comfortable showing myself to people. Always afraid of the looks and jaw dropping. Know what I'm sayin', good chap?"

"I hear ya buddy. It's hard to trust people 'dese days. Sometimes I feel better off by my lonesome."

"Me too. Glad I found you to hang with though. Say George, I've got a secret to tell ya, but ya can't tell anyone, no matter what. Deal?" Arthur extended his hand to George for a shake.

"Yup, you can trust me." And the two shook on it.

George, a little antsy to hear the secret, began to get excited. He felt this would be a turning point in their friendship. George never really had a close friend; a friend with whom he could share things and George was always looking for someone to share his secrets too.

"George, back in Alaska... well, back there... I killed a man. Took his life right from him."

George seemed unfazed by this proclamation. "Just da one?" George said jokingly.

"Nope, several." Now curious, George wanted more information. "Why'd ya do it Arthur? How'd ya do it?"

"Just needed to relieve stress and they picked on me too. Not physical abuse. I can damn sure handle my own, but emotional and mental abuse that lead to anguish. I felt, uh, what's those words – oh yeah anxious, confused, and belittled. Made me feel less than nothin' is what my shrink told me anyway. Know what that's like George, to feel like less than nothin'?"

"Yup, sure do."

While George understood, he was not willing to divulge his personal demons as to why he knew or understood Arthur's plight.

110

"George, here's another confession. I've done bad things here in Louisiana, too." "Hmm, ya don't say." George said unsurprised.

"Yeah, I've done the same thing right here in this little town. People just think

I'm different and I hate it."

"Yeah, I hate it when it happens like 'dat with people. Makes me angry too,

Arthur."

"Agreed young fellow. Aaagreed!"

"Hey, I gotta get to runnin'. I have a few errands to get done before it gets too late."

The night sky was low and cloud cover loomed as the smell of rain filled the air.

George sat on the park bench waiting for Arthur. He waited, and waited, and waited some more. George had nowhere to go, but was sick of waiting. He began to walk and in the distance he heard a faint noise. He couldn't tell what it was; however, he thought it resonated like metal clanging on rocks. He was drawn closer to the muffled noise. He silently hid behind a tree and peeked around the safe haven to see Arthur digging a hole underneath the bridge. Next to Arthur was a motionless figure. George moved closer, but was careful not to alarm Arthur.

"Psst, Arthur," George whispered just loud enough to be heard by Arthur's big ears.

Arthur spun on his big feet and peered at George with intent and desire. Fire built in his eyes like a burning ember. The steam came off his body in the cool night air like smoke erupting from a volcano.

"Whoa! Arthur, it's me, George."

"Ah, George good buddy. How ya doin' 'ol chap? Sorry 'bout that, you startled me a bit."

"Whatcha doin', Arthur?"

Arthur now had his back turned to George and

111

offered little suggestion to why or what was happening; almost in a trance, Arthur went back to digging.

"Hey Arthur," George squeaked out, still peering from the safety of the tree.

George saw Arthur again spin around, but this time he appeared like Lucifer and attracted a reddish glow.

"Damn George, I thought ya left."

"No, I'm still here. Whatcha doin' over 'dere, Arthur? Can I help ya?"

A long sheepish grin overtook Arthur as he slowly lifted his giant head to George.

Motioning George to come on over, Arthur turned to begin digging again.

"George, this is Jeff Langburger. Langerstein? Langerburgerstein? Lang-somethin or other. Jeff, this is George Tate. He's my friend. Don't worry George; Jeff is dead so he won't be doing much talkin'. He and his friends were walking through the park and he dropped back to have a piss. He saw me and laughed so I killed him. Had a helluva time too. That bastard's at least six feet tall. I had ta jump from a tree branch and I ended up slicing his head clean-off. Did it in one blow too. Made it real easy to drink his blood straight from that vein popping out, right there." Arthur pointed to Jeff's beheaded neck and jugular still throbbing.

"George, you okay? You're not sayin' much."

George was actually unfazed by the entire incident, but Arthur took the non- emotion as disgust.

"George, you understand? It happens. People see me, make fun of me, and I can't handle it. I snap."

"Arthur, Arthur," George waved his hands, palms facing Arthur, "Ya don't need to explain it ta me. I get it! Give me 'dat shovel. You gonna need a bigger hole. He's a bigun."

George grabbed the shovel from Arthur and started digging. The two discussed the intricacies of being different from what people expected.

"Been picked on most of my life, Arthur. It started way back in grade school and just kept comin'. Not sure why. Think it's the way I talk or the way I just am. Don't know though."

"I hear ya, chap. With me, it's the little thing. People see me and want to have gawk. Pisses me off really."

"Yeah, I thought you was interesting looking from the get go. Never really minded it though, ya know."

"Never really minded it? Well goddamn, I hope not or I'd have to give ya a whack." Arthur said as he hit the ground hard with his large foot and sinisterly smiled.

"Yeah, whatever," George retorted with a laugh.

As the looming rain made a brief appearance, Arthur told George of his past encounters and surmised that the two weren't much different.

Arthur bluntly started, "So this bastard hears me in the bushes five nights ago. He thinks it's a cat and starts to throw rocks. Prick hits me in the head. I obviously can't back down so I leap from the bushes and scare the shite straight outta him. He stood speechless, open-mouthed, and shaking all about. I clocked him a good one with my stick and down he went like a sack-a-potatoes. Think you'd a done the same too, George."

George, still digging, nodded favorably. The hole was finally large enough to accommodate Jeff, and the two roughly tugged and pushed until Jeff's limp body fell into the dark abyss. George kicked the head in and it made a thud on the limp corpse. After Jeff was covered with dirt and rocks, Arthur pointed off in the distance, on the other side of the road, "Three buried there."

"I'm not just a watcher, ya know. Hit a guy with a rock a few years back in a fight. Blood gushed everywhere. He kicked and wriggled on the ground so I hit 'em a few more times until his eyes closed," George

113

admitted while getting a good hold on the shovel.

"Hmm. Ya don't say."

"How many ya think it's been, Arthur"?

"Not sure anymore, good fellow. Ya lose track after the first dozen or so."

"Mornin' gonna come quick and I best be goin' to get a start on my weekend errands. I'll see ya later, Arthur."

George didn't see Arthur that night. George didn't see Arthur the next night or the night after that either.

*****

It was a Friday night with the chill of autumn in the air and the full moon had dipped behind cloud cover. The moon peaked out, offering a pale light through a blanket of shrouded clouds.

As the dirt pile became a bit larger and slightly higher with every drop from the shovel, George stood up to stretch and arch his back. He'd done this too many times and knew better than to bend and roll his back. *Use your legs and waist, he insists.* No one was in sight and the wee hours made certain that no one would see the evil that lurked in George Tate's backyard on this, the demon's night.

Suddenly, George heard a low groan coming from the very short, twice-folded over, black bag lying in the darkness near the wooden fence. He casually walked over, offered a solid kick from the steel toe of his heavy work boot, listened, then heaved back and smashed the metal flat head of the shovel several times on the wriggling object in the highly tear-resistant bag. He bent down and flipped the oversized foot back into the bag and zipped it shut. George then went about his business in his back yard.

*****

"Dunno." Detective Gamble replied when asked why they haven't found any more bodies in the city.

"Maybe he moved to another city or somethin'," Larson added.

"Yup. Maybe. Or, maybe he's just takin' a solid break."

"Ya know what's not takin' an effin break? This damn weather! Hot as Hades out 'der."

# The Red Coat

The road twisted and turned as he drove his car down the mountain. With not a headlight in site, Zack took the short line speeding through every turn. The path was filled with "S" curves and right angles. He eased off the gas and then slowly pressed the pedal as his high-performance engine responded accordingly. He cornered with careful precision piloting his matt-black Maserati through and around every bend on the mountainous road. His car could do zero to sixty in just four seconds.

Zack always dreamt of owning a fast car and once he became a big shot lawyer he made his dream come true. The Mas was the fastest car he could afford. He loved the feel of the hand-stitched soft-leather steering wheel. The shifter knob fit perfectly in his hand at the change of every gear. The engine was smooth and married in perfect harmony to speed and performance. It was as though the car was specifically built for Zack.

The steep road had only a thinly veiled metal guardrail to keep speed and fiber in tact. One's mind could not wander when driving the treacherous terrain. "Hi honey," Zack shouted while zipping from his hilltop cabin.

"Hey baby. How was your quiet getaway?"

"It was great to be in the woods for a few days, but the power went out twice. I need to get a generator up here for next time. Anyway, I just wanted to say that I'm on my way and I should be home in a few hours."

"Okay sweetie. I'll see ya soon. Be careful driving. Ta-ta." And with that, Zack was disconnected from his beautiful bride-to-be.

Zack pressed his hands-free button on his Italian leather steering column and continued to speed home. All Zack had to guide his way were his xenon cluster lights throwing a bright and clear beam. He enjoyed that the lights automatically tracked the movements of the steering wheel so that the beam pointed to the inside of a curve.

Bends turned everywhere on the road. Lights shifting with every turn, Zack became mesmerized by the twisting road, but pressed even faster. The sign read: *Slow, curve ahead.* Zack knew his Blakcat, as the license plate read, could handle the bend with ease. With his foot on the gas, he confidentially sped around the inside line.

In a single, but late reaction, Zack stood on the brake and almost instantly screeched to a skidding stop. He was caught in a slow motion process that would change his life forever. He could feel the brakes grab, but he plowed through the person standing in the road.

From the front of the car, a body flipped up, slid off the roof and over the back of the car. The sports suspension dug into the frame of the car and the jolt sent Zack's head bouncing off from the airbag and against his headrest. Smoke and dust filled the air surrounding the car. The fresh smell of burnt rubber filled Zack's nostrils. He checked his faculties, shook his head and realized that, minus a few scratches, he was in good condition.

He cautiously opened his door and, using his cell phone as a light, immediately went to assess the damage to his baby. The front end showed a crease halfway up the hood. The roof only had a few scratches and the back end showed no harm. A hesitant sigh of relief slowly developed within Zack.

He took a deep breath and looked on the road for the splotch of red that he saw briefly in the corner of his eye. Zack walked back down the road almost a half-mile, but found nothing. No red clothing, no person, nothing.

*Whoever was wearing that red coat surely went over the guardrail and plummeted to his or her death,* he thought.

Zack took a few more deep breaths, and then

shakily walked to the edge and looked over. *It's gotta be over three hundred feet down there!* He peered into the darkness but not even the stretch of moonlight strewn enough for him to see any hope of life.

"Anyone down there? Anyone? Can – you – hear – me?" He hopelessly yelled into the abyss while cupping his hands around the sides of his mouth.

Zack dropped his head and made his way back to his banged and dented machine. The airbag now fully deflated, Zack gingerly slid into the driver's seat and slowly pressed the ignition button.

First try, the car gave a puhVRooPuHoo puhVROOpuhHOO and misfired. A second push of the start button offered up the very familiar vooRRRvooRRRvooRRR as Zack gave his baby fuel-injected power, the engine turned over. Zack adjusted his rearview mirror, took a look and he could feel his heart skip a beat.

He took another quick look and spun his head around to look over his shoulder as he thought he saw a person standing behind his car. *Uhhh, holy shit. That scared the crap outta me!* He said out loud. Realizing it was only his imagination, he slowly and gradually drove off.

Zack kept telling himself that it was a deer, but he knew differently. He kept thinking that if he told himself the same story over and over, soon he'd believe it as truth. *It was a deer. It was a deer. It was a deer!* He repeated. He made his way home that night and the second he walked in the door he told his girlfriend that he had hit a deer. He took his car to get repaired and the dealership never questioned anything or asked any questions. Zack felt that he was in the clear.

A few months passed and Zack saw nothing in newspapers or online about a person getting hit or killed while on the Sinamore Valley Road near Kilamen. He checked daily. More months passed and still nothing.

Zack began to have strange dreams. It was always the same: Zack was sitting in his wrecked car and saw a man in a red jacket walking towards his car. The man was limping, dragging his right leg. His left arm was clinging to his right pant leg while pulling it when he walked.

His right arm was beckoning in a slow circular motion. Zack couldn't hear anything, but he saw the man's lips moving and he could visibly see and read the words, "Help me! Help me! Please!" In the dream, Zack drove off and saw the man in front of his car with his hands out in front of him as if to stop the car from hitting him. It was the same dream and Zack woke up in a cold sweat while his heart beat heavy and his pulse raced fast.

Zack couldn't sleep, afraid of what he would see. He stole naps in his office. During one nap, Zack relived his drive that fateful night. Instead of not finding the body, Zack dreamt that he actually pushed the lifeless body over the edge of the cliff and heard the words, "Noooo! Dooooonnn't!" as he rolled the person off the edge. Zack woke in his comfy plush leather chair screaming silently.

He couldn't get the image of that red jacket out his mind. He saw it all too often, the full moon in the backdrop, the pale white face, the red jacket, the figure waving arms as to bring Zack's roaring car to an abrupt stop. He contemplated and struggled his emotional guilt. He convinced himself he could hear a voice yelling out just before impact. The more he thought it, the more deafening it got.

*****

This just in from 36 News at Nine: A gruesome discovery by state troopers along Hwy 97 in Sinamore Valley just outside of the city of Kilamen. We go live to Chet Blatherton on the scene.

"Jackie, gruesome barely describes the sight of this

119

terrible murder. State police have confirmed that a man has been killed after he was carjacked at an intersection near Kilamen. All police have to go on is a few seconds from a traffic camera. Other details are sketchy at best; however, it is evident that the man driving the car wore a red jacket and was pushed from the driver's side of the car. Video shows that the carjacker jumped out of the car and repeatedly struck the driver over the head. He then stripped him of the red jacket and that's when the grisly murder took place. We're not gonna show it here, Jackie. It was just too violent. I'm Chet Blatherton, live near Kilamen. Back to you, Jackie."

"Wow, did you hear that, sweetie?" Claire asked her man.

"Geez, that's terrible. Who'd do such a thing?" Zack asked.

The mere mention of the red jacket brought memories racing back. Now he wondered to himself if it was just coincidence or did the person actually survive being hit only to realize a horrific death months later? Zack shook it off and surmised that there's more than one red jacket in the world.

Three months later the couple were at the cabin, when the knock came.

"Honey, who in the world could that be?" his girlfriend asked.

"Dunno! I mean it's ten o'clock and co-o-old out." Zack opened the door to see a stranger standing in front of him wearing a red coat.

Zack turned three shades of pale. Blood was slowly being drained and his hand went limp from the doorknob. His mouth opened as if his jaw had come unhinged. He could feel a cold sweat rapidly protrude from his forehead. He went numb and froze in place like a statue. The man at the door had his head down looking at the ground.

"Howdy, think I could use you're phone? My car stalled just about a quarter mile away." The stranger said without lifting his head.

Zack was beyond stunned as his mind raced and contemplated if this red-coated man was the person that was hit or the car-jacker...or just a stranded motorist. "Uh...just a second!" Zack blurted and unapologetically slammed the door. He reached for his cell phone and yelled to Claire, "I'll be on the porch, hun." Zack opened the door cautiously to see the stranger patiently waiting.

"Sorry about that, had to grab the cell," Zack explained to the hood-wearing visitor. "Where'd it stall?"

"Um, 'bout quarter mile back down the road. Not too many houses 'round 'dese parts are 'dere?" The man responded in a gravely smoker's voice.

"Yeah, neighbors are few and far between out here," Zack replied nervously while trying to get a good look at the face in the dark only a few feet away.

"Tell ya what, hearing 'dat news on 'da radio about some murderer on 'da loose; I'd rather be here on 'da phone 'dan on 'dat road," the stranger said.

"Oh yeah, I heard it on the news. Nasty stuff."

"Yup. I mean, think 'bout it. Some fella just lopped of 'dat guys head for nothin'. Who does shit like 'dat?"

The man dialed and got a busy tone. He hit the call button again and nothing happened.

"Hey," Zack sensing the problem immediately interrupted the caller. "Yeah, there's not a very strong cell signal around here. Maybe walk out a bit away from the house. That might work." Zack added while pointing down toward the road.

The visitor moved off the porch steps and attempted his call again, his back to the house. Meanwhile, a sudden rush came over Zack. Sweat trickled down the back of his neck, while at the same time his breath was crystallizing in the cold air. Zack wanted to know who this guy was

121

and why he was *really* at the house. Confusion and paranoia grabbed Zack's mind.

In a blur of rage mixed with insanity, and fueled by sheer anxiety, Zack lunged at the man, throwing his open hands around the man's neck. The force knocked the stranger face down onto the semi-frozen ground. Zack was relentless and added force to his throttling choking spree, grabbing every breath from his victim until the man's feet stopped kicking.

*****

Breaking news from 36 News at Nine: "We go live again to Chet Blatherton..." "Thanks Jackie. New details have emerged about today's carjacking and homicide near Kilamen. Officers have reported that the grainy video footage that showed, albeit briefly, the carjacking and murder was altered from its original format. A police investigation has shown that the murder victim was actually the carjacker. You heard that correctly, the driver of the car seemingly fended off his attacker and in the process killed the assailant. Police are still looking for the silver Mercedes and the driver or owner of the car. Video shows that he's wearing a red coat. I'm Chet Blatherton, 36 News at Nine."

Claire opened the front door to see a body on the ground. Her fiancé was standing off to the side clutching a red jacket and breathing heavily.

"Hello, 9-1-1. What's your emergency? Hello? Hello?" Asked the operator on the phone, which was lying on the ground near the stranger's head.

## I See the Light

Shortly after joining the dark side, as he comically referred to his blindness, Alan Gerald went through the various stages of denial and depression. He couldn't believe that it had happened to *him*. He would tell his close friends that it didn't make sense, "There are people out there much worse than me, like, real mean people. Murders, rapists... why not them?" He would ask in frustration.

The anger overtook him and he would go into mad fits. He would yell at people on the street and use his disease against them. "See the stick? It's got a red tip. Yeah, I'm blind. Get outta the way," he would say as he erratically bounced his white cane.

He regularly negotiated with the god of his choice, any god who would listen, "Just let me see. I beg! One, maybe a few years..." he said while on is knees beside his couch. He got to the point where depression paralyzed him.

He dreaded having to get out of bed every day, rarely brushing his teeth or changing his dirty clothes. He lived like a recluse and a shut-in. He couldn't wait to get back into his bed at night after a tough day of self-loathing. He gravitated to marijuana – lots of it – to cope and get through the whys of why *he* went blind.

In his darkness, Alan keenly developed his senses of touch, smell, and hearing. He began to lean on those faculties in his world.

After seven years of being unable to see, Alan's parents passed in a tragic crash while on their twentieth wedding anniversary. He was left with his trusty companion and friend, his dog, Tank. Tank was a brute of a Seeing Eye dog, half protector, half guide, and all brawn. The big American bulldog was the first of his breed to become a guide dog. Al was a sight to behold when walking down the sidewalk with his cane in one hand and his other loosely holding the lead for his somewhat bow-legged, muscular black-and white spotted friend.

*****

"Nice Harley!" Alan shouted enthusiastically toward the sound of the bike. "Thanks, man." The voice yelled back.

"What color is it?" Al asked with his eyes hidden behind dark sunglasses.

"What? Man, are you kiddin' me?" The rough voice shouted back over the roar of the engine.

Alan walked near the bike, extending his hand into the air to shake the rider's hand, "Sorry, man, I'm blind. I used to ride."

"Oh! Oh! Sorry 'bout 'dat, man. I had no idea." The man said as he shook Al's hand.

"No prob, man."

"I'm Joe. Joe Johnson. My buddies call me Mean Joe. Here, check it out. It's black and dark green. They call it metallic green." Joe said as he reached for Alan's arm to guide him to the bike.

Al ran his hands over the beach-style handlebars, felt the flowing steel, and down to the leather-stitched seat. He reminisced about his own bike back in 1986. He remembered his '85 Harley Davidson Sportster. Etched in his memory—the curvature and clean lines of the custom chrome exhaust. He often thought it flowed like the breeze on a cold winter day. He could see the vivid purples of the frame and front fork, matched against the magenta inlay with onyx undertones on the large gas reservoir. The front and back fenders matched the beautiful tank.

He envisioned the front suspension, designed for easy riding and comfort, as the bike would roar down the road. With a bit of imagination, he could feel the wind pushing his cheeks back and the gyration of his arms through his triceps while riding the open highway.

"Man, I loved being on the road. Nothin' but an open space. It was like a painter's canvas to me. I would ride a straight line, zig-zag, or even do slow rolls from side-to-side. I miss it! I really do. It was...it was just freedom." Hearing the desire in Alan's voice made the burly and intimidating Joe well up a bit, but he didn't crack.

Joe Johnson reached into his back pocket and pulled out his sterling-silver, chained wallet and handed Alan a business card. It read Joseph Johnson, Esquire.

"Give that to someone who can read, uh, sorry. I mean who can drive you. Give me a call and we'll ride." Joe told him, in a suddenly professional and clear manner. Mean Joe Johnson had an alternate life: mild-mannered during the week and wild biker on the weekends.

"That's so cool!" Al shouted as he later handed the card to his friend Terry.

A few weeks passed and Alan made plans to meet Joe for a ride. Terry dropped Al at Mean Joe's and as soon as he stepped out of the car, Alan could hear the roaring twin-cam engine as Joe laid into the throttle as a greeting for Al.

"Hey Alan! I'm straight back in the driveway, 'bout fifty feet. There's nuthin' in yur way but cement, buddy."

Alan, with a helmet in-hand, swaggered toward the sweet smell of exhaust fumes until he could feel the heat given off from the engine.

"Where we headin' today, Mean Joe?" Alan asked with unabashed eagerness.

"Thought I'd hop on Country Pass, head to North Lake, then ride the Double Mountain back the long way, and then through the city back home. Whadda ya think *Big A*? I gotta give ya a biker tag." He said with a rumbling laugh.

Alan laughed a bit at his new nickname. "Sounds fantastic!" he shouted over the screaming of the bike.

The ride was long, but Alan enjoyed the freedom that only a motorcycle could offer. He felt every twist and turn of the roads. It all came back to him – the flow and movement, the ease of motion. He could sense and leaned into every tilt of the bike at the appropriate time. The weight of his black leather jacket as the wind forced it against him, the sounds of the rubber on the road, even thud of the tiny bugs hitting his helmet; for the first time since his disease had struck, Alan felt alive.

The bikers stopped at Lucy's Looky Lookout on the top of Double Mountain for a quick stretch and a Coke before descending into the hustle and bustle of city riding.

"So, how'd, uh...well, "

"How'd I go blind?" Alan asked with a smirk.

"Yeah, how'd ya go blind?"

"Stargardt's Disease. It's an inherited macular degeneration, which deteriorates
the sight and eventually leads to blindness. Finally took effect when I was about twenty. Happened later than it should have."

"Oh. So one of your parents..."

"Naw. I thank my grandpa for it." He said, laughing.

"So, it's been almost twenty years then, huh?"

"Yup. Ya know, I got stuck on the things I lost without sight, instead of looking to what I would gain through an increase of my other, seldom used senses. Took a while." "Man, I can't even imagine."

"This though, the motorcycle; the ride; the breeze; the air; just being out here able to...this is one of the thing's I missed most. I was lucky, ya know, with the progression of the disease. It usually develops and people

126

become increasingly limited over a short period of time. Mine was opposite."

"I don't know, it sounds tough, but it sounds like you've handled it well, too."

"Yeah, wasn't always that way. I slooowly began to accept it and, well, even embrace it. I remember telling a friend back then, 'Ya know, this is good. I'll concentrate on other things and maybe even help others afflicted.'"

"Did you, help others?"

"I did. Like I mentioned, it usually hits fast and people who get the disease are typically blind around thirteen at the oldest. I worked with the younger kids. Took my dog too. They loved him."

"Well, ya know, we should hit the road. Whaddya say?" Mean Joe suggested. "Sounds good. Lead the way."

"Hey, Al, the ride down goes fast, but I'll take it easy for ya so you can enjoy the road. I'll give ya a leg tap when we hit the bottom." Joe said with an unseen grin.

It wasn't until Alan was nearly forty when he met Joe Johnson. Mean Joe, as he was commonly called in his biker circle, was the quintessential motorcycle guy. He was big and burley with a deep gruff voice. Joe wore his beard long, and his graying whiskers were a stark contrast to his black leather jacket. His denim blue jeans showed a few tatters and his thick-soled black biker boots completed his tough-guy-biker persona. Joe was the kind of biker who would never imagine having anyone ride bitch on his bike...until he met Alan.

The two met outside the Amoco station when Al got out of his friend's car to "see" the bike rumbling at the pump next to him.

Mean Joe mounted his bike and Al followed as the two headed off to the bottom via the curvy, spiraled road. The ride down took about twenty minutes and Alan enjoyed every minute of peacefulness; no traffic, no other sounds but the roar of the engine, the tires churning up asphalt, and the whoosh of the wind over his helmet. Suddenly, he was jolted from his solitude by a thump on the leg. That was his cue that the bright lights and big buildings were ahead.

After riding for nearly thirty years, Mean Joe Johnson could handle a bike like most handle a toothbrush – without thought, but with straight instinct. Weaving in-and- out of traffic and changing lanes was second nature. He knew it was better to be seen rather than think you're seen.

Joe peeked over his shoulder, gracefully pressed, then leaned left to change lanes. He watched on his left as a red pickup narrowly missed a car after changing lanes. Joe could see that the driver of the truck was messing with the radio and talking to the passenger. Joe saw the traffic ahead and decided on his proper lane to avoid any interference. He slowed the bike for traffic, then sped up to work the motorcycle over one more lane to the far left.

The speeding pickup jammed its way ahead of the other cars and ended up two cars ahead of Joe and Al, but one lane over. The driver decided to squeeze ahead of the car he'd been tailgating and collided with another car changing lanes simultaneously. The two crashed in a fury of metal and anguish, sending both flipping and rolling after a violent overcorrection of the steering wheel. The traffic screeched, but more cars got involved in the wreck.

Mean Joe immediately grabbed at the brake levers and tried to maneuver the heavy machine toward the shoulder of the highway. The wide back tire threw into a skid and the bike went sideways. The front end of the catapulting truck slammed into the front wheel and fork of Joe's motorcycle.

Flames crackled and plumes of thick black smoke spiraled through the air as people got out of their cars in bewilderment and awe. The putrid smell of burning rubber permeated the air. Mean Joe was trapped, struggling under the weight of the front of the pickup, near the barren rim. He wriggled and flailed about, hoping someone would see his pains and fight with the metal monster.

Just as a man wearing an orange safety vest made a move toward the truck, a three-car chain reaction caused a ferocious crash jolting the truck forward. Joe's twitching movements and arms stopped. The bare wheel suddenly lurched as the rider's helmet rolled away with a thick sanguine trail following with each rotation. The sounds of crushing bone would scar the squeamish.

The vested man turned his attention to the helmeted passenger who was thrown from the bike. "Can you hear me? Mister, can you hear me?" He yelled over the commotion, without response. He reached for the limp wrist and could feel a pulse. He was careful not to move the man who was dressed in black leathers. "HEY!" he shouted to whoever was listening, "call an ambulance. NOW! This one's alive. HURRY!"

Completely unconscious and unresponsive, Alan was rushed to Scarsdale General where he lay in a coma for three days. The ambulance crew found no identification at the scene nor on Alan. He was an unknown. A John Doe.

*****

"Doctor," the nurse shouted down to the main station, "come quickly. He's mumbling! The... John Doe. He's talking!"

"Sir. Sir. Sir." The doctor said softly while gently touching Alan's right arm. Al saw darkness, but this was a different darkness from what he usually saw.

There was a dim light in it. He slowly lifted his eyelids exposing his magnificent blue eyes to his new world.

129

"I can see! I can see!" He groggily mumbled.

"Hello. I'm Dr. Jones."

"I can see you! I can! The light, the walls, you; I can see it all! It's very bright in here, but I can see."

The doctor gave Alan Gerald a confusing look before speaking, "Sir, do you remember being in an accident?"

Alan slowly nodded, while the doctor spoke further.

"Well, do you..."

Before Dr. Jones could explain, Alan interrupted and said, "Please, doctor, call me Al."

"Well, Al, that was next. What is your name?"

"Alan Gerald and I can see everyone in this room!" he joyfully proclaimed. "Uh-ha, um, that's great Mr. Gerald. Can you tell me what you remember from the accident?" The doctor asked while giving a look towards the nurse.

"It was a long day of riding. The mountains; the sounds; the bike; Mean Joe; I remember it all."

"Then what? Do you remember being in an accident?"

Alan nodded accordingly, "Yes."

"What happened?" asked Dr. Jones

"I remember briefly hearing the screeching tires of the cars behind us, and then momentary silence as if the Earth stopped moving and all the people didn't breathe or make a sound. I felt a sudden jolt and then the sensation of being thrown through the air. It was like being on a roller coaster, knowing you'll get to the bottom, but not sure just when. I could actually hear myself land and I felt my body bounce and slide into a barrier. I felt a jolting pain, hurt like a mofo...that's all I remember."

"Well, Mr... sorry, Al, that's enough for now." The doctor said and immediately looked down at the chart.

"Where's Mean Joe? Joe Johnson?" Alan asked.

"I'm sorry, Alan, the other rider didn't make it. He died at the scene."

For a moment, his thoughts drifted to the one man who offered him the feeling and freedom of one last ride. He was able to do something he hadn't done in nearly two decades: staring aimlessly while thinking.

It was as though Alan Gerald forgot he was ever blind. It wasn't until he snapped back to the people in the room and noticed the vibrant red folder in the nurse's hand that he even thought to mention it.

"I was blind!" He blurted out as if it was the answer to the winning question on a TV game show.

"Blind?" The doctor was puzzled.

"Yes, blind. Couldn't see a damn thing! Nothing! I was blind since just after high school. I can see now though!" Alan proudly announced. "I can't wait to do so many things," he rambled, "skiing, driving, hell, even watching TV *and* seeing it. Amazing!"

The doctor walked closer to the bed where Alan lay, still as a breezeless day, looked at the room nurse, and then down to Alan, "Mr. Gerald, I have some bad news. The accident abused your spine and the nerves have become unresponsive. You're paralyzed from the waist down."

## The Big Bad Wolf

The dull, cream-colored, doublewide trailer sat at the end of the lot, bordered by a long irrigation lagoon-style waterway. Wandering canal creatures easily circumvented the shoddy, deteriorating wooden fence that rose about a foot from the ground.

"Can ya git-it out?" Asked the clearly agitated man.

"Yeah. Absolutely! Any idea how long, or about how long it is?" the wildlife removal expert inquired.

"Um, hmmm, uh, well, the pool's about thirty-five feet so I'd say it's maybe ten feet or longer. It's a big 'ol 'gator," the man said, while cautiously walking near the murky blue water of the pool to check on the hulking dark green creature holding steady at the bottom.

"Wow! Okay. We'll be over in a bit."

"Great! Sounds good. I'll be gone, but I'll leave the back gate unlocked," he said as he peeked over the edge one last time to glimpse the dinosaur-like spines of the alligator.

The man with the reptile problem casually walked to the front of his side-by-side trailer and stepped up into his jacked-up, white pick-up truck with a window emblem of a scantily clad women with big boobs and a bumper sticker that read, *Made for Muddin'*. The truck had extra knobby off-road tires set on black on chrome, extremely oversized rims. The bottom of the driver and passenger doors came to just above his waist. At six feet three inches, he wasn't a short person, but even he needed to use the two-step ladder. His pride and joy, as he called it, was the redneck version of the yellow Corvette.

He gripped the hand-written note tightly and closed the door to his pickup. He went through his mental checklist: *duct tape, got it. Knife, right here.* He felt the sheath attached to his snakeskin belt to be reassured. *Oversized potato sacks, in the back. Address, yup.* He glanced at his note from the Internet to make sure he knew where he was going: 1314 Cayman Drive – Ask for Howard.

*****

Howard Schmeckler only remembered answering his front door for the gentleman who was interested in purchasing his red, felt-covered pool table. It was a genuine classic made of a traditional mahogany finish. The Olhausen had solid hard maple rails with round, pearlized sights. Howard recalled telling the man about the piece, how it was made from all American craftsmanship, that it was of an entry-level series; however, it was truly for the discriminating pool player. The last words he heard were: " The beauty and playability of this thing will be used for years to come. It's mint!"

A half full saltshaker of cocaine sat on the dining room table with powdery residue on a dollar bill-sized, non-porous mirror. Next to it lay a shiny, silver box-cutting razor used to thin out and finely grind the coke. The man from Florida showed anything but Southern hospitality when he peered at his subject, sitting across the modern, sheer black expanse of the table top, and then off to the corner, where an extra dinner chair sat, strategically positioned. He raised his right index finger as a thought entered his drug-laden mind, but paused just long enough to forget his idea completely.

The man reached for the blade, sprinkled the powdery coke along the glass, and began to chop erratically. Howard watched in a haze as the man's right hand began to move methodically like a swift machine, reducing the cocaine into a short thin line, moving it about quickly, and creating another equally straight white line.

Howard shook his head free of his induced sleep and observed as the man rolled the dollar bill into an extremely tight cylindrical tube. In one quick motion, he leaned over while placing the dollar in one nostril, held his other closed and inhaled deeply through the free opening causing the whiteness to disappear.

Howard was a skinny, narrow-shouldered man with a receding hairline and all he could do was watch as the man in front of him released nervous energy by pacing and punching the palm of his left hand with a fist made by his right.

"What do you want with me?" He asked meekly through his shaky voice while securely seated in the confines of the high-back, pleather dining chair. White clothesline rope tied his arms to each armrest while three-inch wide, standard gray duct tape secured his legs to the seat posts.

"You're a classic affirmation of everything that is wrong and tainted in America," came the response from the man wearing classic black tactical cargo pants and a pair of thick-heeled, black work boots. His trouser legs were sharply tucked into his footwear. His belt matched his kicks and his shirt was taught and gathered snuggly. His red ball cap was pulled tightly over his shaved head and rested just above his eyebrows. He was combat ready for his own personal war.

Howard looked at the man in black and could make out the lettering "W" is "R" ended with a swastika on his right forearm. His eyes ventured towards the man's face and eventually rested upon his neck where another glaring Nazi symbol had been tattooed just under his right ear.

It was obvious to Howard that his captor espoused the ideology of fascism leaning to neo-Nazism. Sensing the complete irony of the man's statement, Howard decided that if this was his end, he was going out with a bit of wit and a lot of aggravation. "What's your name? I think if you're gonna do something to me, you should at least tell me your name."

"Name's Rowdy. Rowdy Travis. Rowdy, like ass-kickin' rowdiness. What do I call you, Jew-boy?"

"Just call me Howard, and yes, I am Jewish, thank you."

"Hmm, Howard? Know what rhymes with Howard?" Rowdy asked, pacing, but didn't even offer time for a response, "Coward! Think I'll call ya Howie."

"Uh, that'd be fine too. My friends actually call me..."

"Yeah, Howie sounds queer. You queer?" He asked without a response.

Rowdy went to a cabinet drawer and pulled out a large, deep, black container. He gently set it down on the table in front of him, and with an elegance that Howard had not seen from the bald, burley man, he slowly and gracefully removed the lid, spinning it corner to corner with one palm diagonally across from the other. Howard watched as the solid metal lid gave off flashes under the chandelier lights. When the spin was done, Rowdy placed the top of the box upside down on the chair next to him and removed the contents.

Howard saw the silk and nylon stitching, the riveted brass eyelets, and the unmistakable colors of the United States of America's Old Glory. When Rowdy created a wave with the material, Howard could feel the breeze strike his face. He then saw the flag was something altogether different: a large, lifelike blue x-shape in the center, surrounded by red. Inside the shape gleamed the familiar white stars...of the Confederate flag.

Rowdy hesitated after unfolding his precious baby, paused to stare, and then stretched his arm for the Krispy Kreme donuts in the white box with red writing and little green dots next to the shaker. He then reached behind him and flicked a metal ball onto the counter. Howard watched as each silver orb made solid contact and then,

135

from inertia, moved off the preceding ball in Newton's Cradle, one-after-one. Clank, clank, clank.

"Mind if I ask you a few questions?" Howard blurted a bit nervously, but figuring he had nothing to lose.

"Whatchya, a reporter?" Rowdy said with a smile large enough to show that he was missing one lower front tooth. "Yeah, I guess. Might as well."

"How long have you been unemployed?"

"Unemployed? What makes you think that?"

"Well, it's the middle of the day on Tuesday and, well, we're here," Howard said with an intuitive confidence that surprised even himself.

"So I'm unemployed. Big deal! Been that way for a few years, I don't know, probably almost three now," Rowdy said while fidgeting with a small snapped sheath on the side of his belt.

"Let me guess, that's about the time that your views changed to, uh,... the extreme?"

"Yup, seems about right, I'd say. I realized that *certain* people were taking my jobs. MINE!" Rowdy exclaimed as he pounded his fist on the table.

"I'm just taking a wild guess again, so you needed to attach yourself to something? Feel useful and needed? Maybe even blame your inabilities and shortcomings on something or someone?" Howard asked in a mild tone, but knowing full well that he was being condescending.

"Doesn't sound like a question to me. Not sure what it is yur sayin', but it doesn't sound good." Rowdy showed a raised eyebrow and a cocked lip to Howard.

"Sorry, I only meant that you wanted to feel useful, like everyman does, right?"

Howard pressed, with an affable, but loathing look that Rowdy missed. "Yeah, why not, I suppose."

"Rowdy, are you a Christian?"

"Hell yeah! Why wouldn't I be?" Rowdy said

136

unequivocally and so emotionally. "It says in the Bible that you should love your brothers."

"Yeah, I'm not much for readin'." Rowdy said, beginning to fidget again.

"It says that only God should judge other men," Howard said with a brief synopsis of favorable verses from the Good Book.

"I'm not judgin', sunshine. I'm followin' the rules of this great land and honorable nation that my forefathers decided upon when they took land from the Ingin," Rowdy said while he looked upon *his* great flag sprawled out on the table.

"Well, you have me tied up, so I'd think that you're judging me right now." This comment put Rowdy in a frenzy of verbal torment.

"Oh shit brutha, you're one of 'da worst kind. A dirty-assed-gay-faggot-homo-fag. Got it ya Jew kike? Only thing's good about ya is that yur a White." Rowdy scowled.

Howard kept his cool knowing full well that he was not in a situation to be argumentative. He had to rely on reason and understanding and hope it would work in his favor, even though he desperately wanted to plunge a knife deep into Rowdy's chest and twist it mercilessly over and over again.

"Just like when we went after them assholes who drove those planes into our buildins', yeah, that's kinda what I'm doin' here, ya see? If it's one, then it's *gotta* be all of 'em, right? Anyway, that's how I'm seein' it, period." Rowdy said it with anger. He grabbed the chair from the corner and smashed it into the ceramic-tiled floor. "That there's what I think of 'em all." He yelled as he spit on the broken pile of shattered wood.

Howard took a deep breathe, paused, "That's the kind of thinking that starts wars and religious disagreement, which always leads to worldly problems.

Let's be honest, people will never think the same, but we still need to respect the thoughts of others, not share in their beliefs, but have respect nonetheless. Don't ya think, Rowdy?"

"Look, hey, I can eat at those places, you know, Chi-pot-lay and Hu-ang Palace. Just 'cuz I like the food doesn't mean I gotta like the people makin' it. All those little Mexican rascals and their different language; I know them bastards are talkin' shit 'bout me. And those tiny little Asian people, with their fast talk, that dark hair, and those beady eyes; little shits."

"But you like the food and respect how it's made?" Howard asked.

"Yeah, I guess. So the fuck what?"

"Let me ask ya, what about Catholics? Their beliefs are a *bit* different than yours."

"Naw, those people are okay as long as they's white folk. Hell, even got me a

Catholic girlfriend. She's got real big titties too. She's okay, ya know," Rowdy stated as he heaved at a fake set of breasts on his chest.

Just then, Howard heard a loud noise coming from a hallway closet, followed by banging and clamoring. Rowdy leaned, bent at the waist, and looked down and around the corner.

"Ahh shhhhit! Looks like the bastard is awake." Rowdy said as he stammered off down the large, white-tiled, narrow corridor. Howard could hear the echoing clomp of Rowdy's solid, molded heels as he pounded toward the slender door. The wood made a whooshing as Rowdy aggressively opened it and reached in and grabbed the noisy culprit by the yolk of the shirt. He dragged a person, wearing a drab yellow pillowcase over his head, while his legs, tied together, flailed about rubbing and marking the sand-colored walls.

"Uh...?" Howard muttered a little too loudly and in

138

shocking horror.

"Uh what, little Howie?" Rowdy snapped. "This here's Lorenzo. He's got himself a racial handicap," Rowdy said in a serious and declamatory way without even a blink in facial expression. He stopped to catch his breath and then hauled his trophy into another room and closed the door.

Howard waited with anticipation and eagerly wanted to know what was happening in the room. After about five minutes he could hear muffled noises and moving around. He wondered what the commotion was all about. It was about twenty minutes when the clatter stopped and Rowdy appeared with sweat rolling down from his sideburns, onto his cheeks, to his chin and dripping onto his shirt, while he was tightening his belt.

Smiling, laughing, and looking, for the first time relaxed, Rowdy admitted, "He was Italian. Black, I-tal-yan. Wait, Black, I-tal-yan, *and* gay. He was a gay!" He added with enthusiastic disgust. "Yup, I buggered his butthole from behind while I slit his throat. Dead!" Rowdy said as he mocked the slashing of a throat by sliding his finger across his neck.

Howard sat as straight-up as his body would allow and he could feel that pull of the ropes at his forearms and the pressure at his feet and quickly scanned the room for anything that could be used to kill him. He keenly watched as Rowdy, his back to Howard, stood with his hands on his hips and took a few deep breaths to allow his breathing to catch back up, while briefly muttering to himself.

Rowdy quickly spun on his heels and glared at Howard. "What?" Howard asked hoping he didn't already know the answer, while Rowdy just looked him over.

"Just admirin' the shape of yur skull." Rowdy said while twirling the pearlized handle attached to the sharp steel blade of his knife. The end of the haft held a round ball emblazoned with a swastika. Rowdy spun it one more time in his right hand, pointed the tip at Howard, and then set it on the beveled edge of the melamine table top and walked away.

It suddenly started to rain, as it often did in South Florida, and Howard could hear the rain of an Everglades storm pounding on the metal roof of his confines. It had the very familiar sound of French fries being fried in hot oil. Howard decided he would give it one more try with his murderous kidnapper before he walked off too far.

"Do you vote?" Howard blurted, stopping Rowdy in his tracks, as he turned around.

"Hell yeah! Sure do. Why wouldn't I?" He asked rhetorically without knowing it.

"Do you think stupid people should be allowed to vote?" Howard asked, hoping to invoke some thought from Rowdy.

"No way! That's how we get Blacks 'n shit in office."

"You do know we have a Black president, right?"

"Yup, but, guess he's better than the old guy who ran." Rowdy said, unbuttoning his shirt.

Howard began to speculate, turned his head a bit sideways and let loose, "Did you vote for..."

"So what if I did? What if I voted for the Black guy? Who cares? Who really cares?" Rowdy was clearly upset and ambled back towards Howard with one eyebrow raised and a crocked, corner-up lip.

"Look asshole, I've had enough of yur shit and dumbass questions." Rowdy yelled defensively while pointing his left index finger at Howard. "It's done rainin' and I'm goin' for a swim."

"I have to use the bathroom."

"Go in yur pants." Rowdy said while turning away and looking in a hallway wall mirror.

A few minutes later, Rowdy got a whiff of the pungent odor. "Did ya shit yur drawers?"

Howard got red-faced, and shook his head timidly indicating that he did.

"Well, puddin' pants, that's a first." Rowdy exclaimed while shaking his head and snorting in laughter.

Howard just couldn't hold his thoughts in any longer and wanted to point out the shining hypocrisy that was Rowdy's life.

"You know what I appreciate about you, Rowdy? You're not a closet racist. You don't hide your prejudice. You're blatant and in-your-face with your complete disdain and hatred of people who aren't like you. I certainly don't like it, but I appreciate that you have honesty in your misdirection."

"I'm just being honest, I'm, uh, not really knowin' what that all meant."

"I mean, you consider yourself a 'pure' American, white-loving, Jew-and-other- race-hating, Christian who isn't gay, but recently had a full-blown sexual encounter with a man in that room back there. You're extreme hatred for Black people didn't stop you from voting for a Black president. Oh wait, *and* you have indicated that Catholics are definitely inferior to Christians, yet your girlfriend is Catholic; and, both are the same while holding the slightest variance in views and belief. Do you know why you're a hypocrite?" He asked as tiny beads of sweat began to form at his hairline and forehead.

"Again sunshine, I ain't big on no those fancy words 'n shit, but if y'all makin' fun of me then we'll see who has the last laugh after my swim. You 'n me gots to come to 'n understandin,' slick. And here's that understandin,' you're tied up like a pig headin' to slaughter and I'm the butcher. Understand? In the end, we can 'what if' all y'all want, but in the end we are what we are."

"No, we are what we've turned into through misguided beliefs, propaganda of those beliefs, and not being educated in ill-begotten beliefs." Howard retorted.

"Yeah, uh, whatever in the hell that all means 'n shit."

"What if I could get you thinking differently?"

"Well, like I said, I'm not big on all that psychobabble bullshit yur prechin' 'n all, but isn't you wanting me to believe like you kinda like me thinking y'all should think like me?"

"You do make a good point in that one group always thinks and feels strongly that their belief structure should be followed; however, and this would be the key point, I see nothing wrong with certain views that are, may I say 'out there' if those views do not degrade, humiliate, intrude, or even denigrate individuals, races, ethnicities, or the sexes."

"Can't really say as I agree or disagree. Not too certain what it is y'all just spewed out there, Howie. Sounded like a good point, but I ain't really sure. How's about we, uh...what's it they call it? Ya know, when to sides don't know..."

"Agree to disagree?"

"Yeah! That's it. We just gotta agree to disagree." Rowdy laughed while he walked to, and opened his refrigerator, grabbed a silvery-white and red can of Old Milwaukee beer, walked to the table and poked a hole in the top of the can with his knife and slammed the brew shotgun-style. He dropped the blade on the table and went back for another.

Rowdy removed his pants and sauntered to his kitchen and then slid open the large glass door to the raised wooden deck. The pool, an anomaly in his neighborhood, was once the community swimming area; however, the previous owner of the development ran out of money for upkeep so Rowdy had bought the pool on the cheap and erected the wooden enclosure.

The slivered moon cast very little light that night, so Rowdy knew no one would see him skinny dipping. Rowdy Travis took a slight run from the back door and in five steps he was airborne in a half-dive, half-leap which propelled him hands first, followed by his head into the water. With his eyes closed, he could feel his belly skimming the lightly textured cement of the pool bottom.

Meanwhile Howard sat inside, tied to the chair, when he heard the telephone ring, then followed by the click of an answering machine.

"This is Rowdy. I can't git to the phone. Please leave a message." It was followed by a click and Howard sat shaking his head. *Really? An answering machine? Unbelievable!*

"Hey, Rowdy! This is Keith. Sorry to be leaving the message so late, but I called a few times today. Anyway, you called to have me remove the gator from your pool, but when I got there this morning, the gate was still locked. Give me a call and let me know when you have it unlocked. We'll stop by and take care of that nuisance alligator then. Have a great day!"

Howard managed to wriggle his skinny left forearm just enough to loosen the rope from the arm of the old wooden dining chair. He slid his arm free, took a deep breath, extended his arm as far as he could until his fingertips just touched the slender handle of the dagger. He was able to work it towards him until he picked it up and continued to work on the rest of his corded shackles.

His heart pounded and his ears listened for the sliding of the heavy patio door. Not sure what he'd do if Rowdy returned, Howard worked fast, all the time listening with his head tilted sideways.

He wiped his florid face, leaned to the side of his feces-stained throne, and gently peeked around the corner

143

of the wall to steal a look outside. He placed both hands on the table and slowly crept from his seat, while aggressively shaking life back into his legs. He used the table edge for guidance and stability while he maneuvered his way to the kitchen and then to the chest-high window.

His eyes grew large as he peered through the cloudy glass and saw the moon-lit shimmering pool water. He paused, smiled, and in no rush, reached for the beige phone positioned on the wall near the corner of the breakfast nook. "Hello, 9-1-1. What's your emergency? Hello. Hello!"

"Uh—uh, never mind. Sorry, wrong number." Howard said as he hung up the phone and walked to the front door to leave his imprisonment.

### Triple XXXaggeration
The smell of her cigarette filled the air.
"Sexual debauchery?" hell, I didn't care.
A porno queen turns out to be a sudden witch.
If you don't like it, kill the bitch.

"She smokes! Don't get me wrong, she's a looker, but she smokes. EWW, Y-U-U-U-C-K!"

"Mike, Mike," Jerry shook his head, "you're goin' about it all wrong. See, here's the thing pal," he said as he draped his arm around his buddy, "you're lookin' to get over a relationship, not *into* another one. Sex her up and the smoking thing, well...you won't even notice that when her clothes are off."

"Man, you just don't get it! I loved Alice and now it's over. She meant the world to me. I can't just go off and be with another woman just like that. Heck, that wasn't ever me in the first place!"

"She couldn't have been all that since I never even met her. Anyway, dude, you're missing out! I'm gonna go get her then." Jerry exuded enthusiasm and confidence in his upcoming quest of a tall, skinny brunette.

"Please, be my guest." Mike stepped aside and motioned his hand, open and palm up while sweeping his arm aside and upward. "Have fun!"

"Dude, you gotta dangle the carrot, literally and metaphorically," Jerry said while shaking his head and walking off.

Jerry was dressed in a ribbed, white long-sleeved shirt with a black Hugo Boss suit coat against indigo jeans. His tanned chest showed through in the inverted triangle created from his opened, top shirt button.

His hair was perfectly cut to the same length. Spiraled from the back, growing up and out covering his entire head. It was a loose buzz cut at best. If it was ever possible to wear needle-like comb as hair, his was the perfect style. Salt-n-peppery with an overuse of product to complete his hurricane-ready hairdo, Jerry was off in search of a female companion.

His watch reeked of millionaire status while making

only thirty-five grand a year and a simple desire to overspend and rack up credit card debt on materialistic accessories. He played the quintessential ladies' man: willing to listen and readily giving compliments at every turn. He had the words, but was limited in the actions of wooing a woman. When women were involved, he was a three f-er: find 'em, fuck 'em, and forget 'em.

Mike was a romantic. He believed in candlelit dinners, holding hands, long walks, and cuddling together under a blanket while watching a movie. For a man, that usually led to endless jarring from buddies and even the occasional bad relationship while looking for love. As a couple, Mike and Alice were on-again off-again. The last argument twisted the worn, loose dial on their relationship meter back to "off."

He was currently stuck comfortably at the second stage of grief: anger. His bad attitude and sour, woman-hating disposition left him wandering and alone at the bar while his friend was starry-eyed and on the prowl.

"Here we go! It's gonna get lurid," Mike muttered to himself as he watched Jerry hit on a short-haired redhead with marine blue eyes and extremely fake boobs, while her exceptionally muscled boyfriend was off talking to friends at the other end of the bar. Jerry had no idea.

*****

"Ya know, dude, Alice had a few faults: she had a wispy, nasally Jew voice mixed with that god-awful New York accent that could wake the dead," Mike said.

"Yeah man, I really *don't* know. I never met her. You wouldn't let me, um, I mean, ya never brought her around." Jerry said with disinterest.

"She was...I mean, she would shrill my name with...with *that* voice. '*Miiikkeee.*'"

"Yeah, sounds terrible."

He hated that she was late for everything: movies,

147

dates, dinner, cabs, and parties; late for everything. He hated how quickly and uncomfortably she could throw the cold shoulder. He hated that she was indecisive. He hated that she didn't like to have sex. He hated how she would monopolize a conversation by telling him how *it* was; like he even had a choice? He hated that she never did things for him. He hated, well...he hated her! No, he despised the bitch!

It took a break-up for Mike to realize that Alice was not the woman for him, until he reached the bargaining stage of grief. He surmised that he could look past those things, or that he was being a bit unreasonable. *Hey, it's not like I need sex every day. I mean, once a week... okay, a few times a month is good. Isn't it? I can make the decisions for both of us. I can do my own things, I guess. That voice, what about that voice? I can get past it. I can.* All the thoughts and questions, complete with answers, ran through his head.

While on the phone, Jerry realized that Mike was a little depressed and was a no- go for the nightlife, so he recruited his friend, Junior, to go out to the bars.

Having been out for a while, Jerry was a bit tipsy, and his beer goggles made those women he wouldn't normally see as sexual objects attractive to him. His horniness added to it too. The two entered a corner bar and Jerry immediately locked eyes with a longhaired brunette and her friend. Jerry gave Junior a shoulder tap and a head nod to follow and the two casually sauntered over to the ladies.

"Hi, I'm Jerry. 'Dis is my buddy, Junior. Can we buy you ladies a drink?" He asked in his not so subtle Italian accent.

"I'm Alice and this is my friend Margarete. A drink would be lovely."

"Ah, Alice and Margaret. Nice to..."

"It's Margarete, not Margaret. Rete, not Ret."

Margarete, the bleached-blonde with sun crease-lined skin immediately interrupted before Jerry got another word out. "Oh, MargaRETE. Ok. Got it," Jerry said while rumbling for cash to pay the bartender. As Junior and Margarete began their conversation, Alice spun on her bar stool with her back to Margarete. She talked to Jerry; however, talking was not on her mind.

"This isn't my first rodeo, cowboy. How 'bout you saddle me up and take me for a ride," Alice whispered to Jerry with an eyebrow lift of approval while she slid her hand to his.

While grabbing Alice's hand, Jerry gave a wink to Junior that told Junior he was now on his own. The two said goodbye and walked out.

*****

"Hey dude, it's me," Junior said. "How'd it go last night?"

"WOW! 'Dat's about all I can say. Man, she rode me like..."

"Yeah, well, I was stuck talking to her friend last night and she told me that the chick went through a break-up, but was cheatin' on her ex all along. Like cheatin' heavy, bro," Junior said as he interrupted.

"So, what's yur point?"

"Dude, she's banged a lot of dudes. Like, fucked hard! No rubbers. Know what I'm sayin'?" Jerry asked.

"Uh-huh. Hmmm."

Jerry contemplated and waited a few weeks before he made his appointment at the health clinic.

Jerry sat in the doctor's office and stared hopelessly at the poster describing various treatments for sexual transmitted diseases. His eyes darted around the room and with a deep building lump in his throat, he began to read the poster for detection methods for STDs.

He got to Chlamydia and could barley swallow that lump. His palms began to sweat and he felt a flush cross

149

his face. His neck became damp and his legs numb. He sat on the edge of the exam table and said a silent prayer. The doctor casually walked in and told Jerry the news.

"Please drop your pants and underwear."

"Uh, Doc? Hey I was lookin', and...well, is there any other methods..." Jerry stopped mid-sentence as the doctor interrupted him.

"Uh...NO!" She exclaimed.

The pretty physician sat on the rolling stool, slowly slid her long elegant fingers into protective gloves and turned to Jerry holding a twelve-inch, enlarged cotton, swab- tipped, plastic rod in her hand, "I'm not gonna to lie to ya, Jerry, this is gonna hurt." She told him with a smile.

Latex glove on, and with a swift and effortless move, the doctor grabbed Jerry's scared little penis and immediately stretched the shaft. With an even faster move, she not so gently, but ever so slowly darted the end of the plastic rod into his penis and began to scrape the interior wall.

Jerry squealed in blood curdling agony at the instant insertion. The intense, acute, and demanding pain was indescribable. Only expletives left Jerry's mouth and a few tears rolled down his cheeks. As his penis shriveled and turtled to hide, Jerry surmised that long-term, loving relationships might be the best bet for a fruitful life. *This is something I wouldn't wish on my worst enemy.* He thought as he pulled up his jeans.

*****

"Hey man, I just wanted to tell ya that I'm ready to meet some ladies. Let's go out! I've accepted my break-up with Alice..." Mike said.

"Alice? Hey, uh, wait a..." Jerry interrupted his friend. "You got a picture of her?"

# Caught with His Kryptonite

It was just another football weekend Sunday afternoon. Derek Michaels lounged on his black leather sofa watching his beloved team execute a thrilling come-from-behind victory over their archrivals. The excitement of the game led to a few beers and then to surfing the Internet. As he frequently did, Derek hit up a few porn sites for free videos.

One thing led to another, the blinds were drawn, but Derek wanted more than just private time. He began trolling sites for local singles. He wandered to a webpage he saw more than once, TheList.com. It was a quick reference located in his favorites. The website showed local women who would offer their services for accommodating gentlemen. Derek was more than willing to oblige just like he had on several occasions before.

One listing caught his eye. *Petite bundle. Some call me a spinner; some call me a wonder; but you can just call me, Sionna! Like a cute little mouse, I play when the cat is away. A mature woman for the mature gentleman.* The picture showed a petite brunette with a blurred-out face. It was the body type he thoroughly enjoyed, slightly curvy, just a handful of breast, and a tight butt. The tramp stamp was a nice touch and he envisioned it as a potential bulls eye. The add read that she was thirty-five.

The body reminded him of his ex. Shannon Dooling was a polite fourth grade teacher who, most said, was as sweet as candy and as cute as a little kitten. The father of her child would agree, for the most part. He also saw the bad side. Through countless custody hearings, her name-calling, and miserable conversations, he saw a side of her that not one student or parent ever saw. She could be downright mean if the setting called for it.

Derek was a charmer, but slightly rubish in manner. He led a simple life as a financial advisor, not attracting too much attention and staying quiet when needed. He would go out on Friday nights and, with some smiling, a wink or two, and a few compliments, talk his way into the pants of unsuspecting ladies.

*****

The two met at the grocery store when Shannon had asked Derek if he could reach something for her off the top shelf. He asked if that was her usual pick-up line and when they saw one another later in aisle six, they both shared a smile and a quick laugh. When the two bumped carts at the checkout, Derek asked her out for coffee.

The relationship was a whirlwind and took off like a jet. Soon after dating, the couple moved in together. Just after that came the proposal and conception. Shortly after that, the downward spiral and tumultuous break-up, followed by her departure from his house. A few months down the road, their little bundle of joy was born and that led to more bickering and contemplation on who would be the best parent.

During the better part of her pregnancy, Shannon lived in the newly built house of her sister, Krista, and her husband, Luke Smith. The two enjoyed having her stay and did all they could to accommodate. Luke took many business trips, and it gave the sisters time to bond.

Krista new that Derek was the wrong guy for her little sister. She introduced Shannon to open-minded, well-educated gentlemen with advanced careers and future potential, as she called it.

Shannon's passion was education, on both teaching and learning. She pushed forward to complete her Master's degree and didn't miss a beat going after her Doctorate.

Derek, meanwhile, had three things in his life that he loved: his son, weed, and an almost uncontrollable penchant for pussy.

They both had secrets that they chose to keep from

one another, whether it was dating, parenting, or even certain gifts they'd buy the little tyke. Derek kept his tendency to smoke Acapulco gold under restraint and made sure to never smoke before his young child was dropped-off for the day. Shannon kept her sexual urges in constraint and her time at Sex Addicts Anonymous extremely private. The couple never had sex after the split.

Derek made feeble attempts to reconcile through drunken emails and emotional text messages, but it was to no avail as Shannon either ignored them or politely said that she was only interested in what was best for their son and being together was not it. That didn't keep him from fantasizing about his ex from time-to-time.

He liked to imagine her naked. It had been almost seven years, but he vividly remembered what it was like to take her from behind over the back of the couch while fondling her boobs or watching his shaft go to work.

He glanced back at the picture of the lady online. He made the call from his *special* phone and the two agreed to meet at her hotel room in the city in one hour. Michaels popped a blue pill and showered eagerly. He spent extra time manscaping to be sure he wasn't too hirsute. It was a twenty-minute drive, which gave the little triangular tablet plenty of time to work.

He weaved his silver Pontiac in and out of traffic on his way to the Best Eastern motel, downtown. He grabbed a few breath mints just before getting out of his car. He ran through his mental checklist: *Mints - check*, as he swirled them around in his mouth.

*Cash - good*, as his hand slipped into his right pant pocket. *Extra large condom - yup*, as his left hand dove into his other pant pocket. *Oh yeah, gotta call to let her know I'm here.* He reached into his back pocket for his phone.

Derek always used a prepaid cell for these types of

153

things, as did most of the ladies whom he called. It was the *business* protocol. He did the same when calling his Mary Jane dealer. He surmised that, just in case police were to get involved, they'd never have his name or *real* telephone number. He made three calls, but the calls went straight to an automated voice message system. He was determined to do his thing so he hurriedly shot off a text message that simply read, "I'm here!"

"Room 512 sweetie. Come on up!" came the almost instant reply that made his phone vibrate uncontrollably. He sauntered over to the elevator, trying to be nonchalant and not too eager. He wanted to look like he belonged and knew where he was going. He rode the elevator solo, and it gave him a moment to adjust. Just the slightest prod and his warlord was soon standing at full attention.

The doors opened and he looked for the sign to direct him. He spun off to the left and walked down the hallway, dragging one finger along the wallpaper border, mimicking the wavy action of the design.

The carpeted hall wasn't overly lit, but by no means dark enough for complete anonymity. He hoped the woman's face was as good as the rest of her body. He had a quick thought of turning back or opting for the staircase and departing.

Derek fought off the urge to leave and casually strolled down the corridor toward ecstasy to squash his growing desire and sexual appetite. He quickly wondered if she would do anal, then his mind diverted to oral.

He loved the scent of a freshly cleaned twat and the gustation of the sweet secretions from a lady's vagina. He made another adjustment, more of a checking to see if he was hard. His anticipation mounted as he coolly knocked on the door.

It cracked open about an inch and all he could see was a blank void. The very dim lighting made the room almost fully dark, hotel-room dark. She told him to come

154

in and get comfortable. He walked to the bed and began to take off his shirt. He caught a brief glimpse of the tiny-framed female's leg as she darted into bathroom. He figured that the woman was so short that she couldn't even reach up to the peephole.

While he was undressing, and with his back turned, she sauntered out in thigh- high black stockings and a red miniskirt. She wore a black bustier with sequin buttons. She was dressed how he would have liked, if he had a chance to see her. He always dreamed of a dirty teacher-type, a bit of a bookworm slut.

She moseyed over to him and slipped her hands around his waist and slowly moved them to his...

He smiled and turned, "Krista!"

## You Look Familiar

He sat alone at the bar drinking his frosted mug of plain light beer and with forty varieties on tap, it was the most vanilla selection he could have picked. He watched as the frozen pieces made their way into the frothy beer and created an amber-colored alcohol slushy. He looked around at the people and curiously wondered if he would find a Ms. Right-for-the-moment. The more he drank those ice-cold brews, the easier it got.

"Hey, howya doin' bro?" The black, leather jacket-wearing man said to him as he sidled up to the long wooden and lacquer-covered bar and took the seat one away from the guy.

"Good," Eric said as he took a long, deep-gulping drink of his Bud Light and turned to mind his own business. *Is this a gay bar? Hmm. That was weird,* he thought.

Eric swiveled on the barstool and noticed a voluptuous, longhaired brunette walking toward him. She had very light curls in her soft hair. She wore metallic and glitter-coated leather high heels.

Her skirt was light brown and hit just below her thigh. Her acrylic sweater was just tight enough to show off the full form of her large breasts. He watched as she swung her purse up on the bar as she plopped down on the stool between the two men. She turned away from Eric and began talking to her friend.

Eric could smell the aromatic pleasures of her perfume and shampoo as she spun away. He ogled for a second and then got back to his beer, but managed to sneak a few peeks too.

As she flagged down the bartender, Eric couldn't help but notice her face. He thought she looked familiar, but he simply couldn't place her. She caught him looking,

"Uh, may I help you?" she asked.

"Oh, uh...no. I'm sorry," he said frazzled. "It's...it's just that you look like someone
I know," he said, embarrassed and flustered while he turned back to his hibernating beer. "Oh, okay," she said, but it was all she could get out before his head turned from her face. *He's kinda cute. A bit strange, but in a boyish kinda way. Nice hair too,* she thought.

"Well, anyway, like I was saying, there we were in the back lot. He threw me up on the hood of the Corvette and right before he was ready to dive in, a duck waddles outta the bushes. A duck! Can you believe it? The entire crew started laughing." She explained to her well built friend sipping his Jack and Coke.

"Wish I coulda seen that one!" he said as he threw back the rest of his drink while motioning for another. "Ya know, the strangest thing that ever happened to me was when I was going at it over the back of a couch and the damn thing broke. Needless to say, she got all of me when we fell." He told her with a devilish wink.

"That's good stuff! I'd love to see a bloopers of sex reel," she added as Eric's neck stretched as far as it could. He suddenly remembered where he'd seen her: porn. She was a porn actress, but her name escaped his sex-enthralled mind. Over the next forty-five minutes, he listened intently to their conversation.

"So that's it, it's settled," she said as she started to grab for her purse. Eric sensed that if he was going to have any chance, it was now. He turned, hoping to catch her gaze.

"Hi. Ya know, it hit me," he said it with a laughing smile that caught her by surprise. "I'm Eric." He said as he extended his right hand for a proper introduction.

"Hello, Eric. I'm Sophie."

"So that's you're real name too?"

"Yeah, it is. It's just my last name that's made up." She told him with a grin. "I know, it's hard to believe that

Suckett isn't my real last name," she added with a sly wink.

"This is corny, but could I take a quick picture with you?" he asked while shaking his phone for her to see.

"Sure, Eric. That'd be cute." He stood next to her with one arm around her and held his cellular out in front of them and tapped the camera button to snap a photo. As her arm dropped, Eric could feel her hand lightly drift over his buttocks. She held it there briefly, gave a gentle squeeze, and then a little slap as she smiled at him. *Holy shit! What's that mean? It's gotta mean something.* His imagination ran free from its constraints.

Sophie returned back to her fizzy cocktail and took a sip. "This is my friend Dick," she said as she was turning to Eric. "He's in the business too."

"Oh, hey, nice to meet you, man." Eric said with a universal head nod since it was too far of a reach to shake hands.

Dick gave a gentle elbow nudge to Sophie's forearm. "Well, whaddaya think?"

"Yeah, yeah-yeah." She responded and took another drink of her spritzer and then spun to face Eric with her enormous boobs and cavernous cleavage leading the way.

"I just read that the neurological effects of chocolate include abnormal behavior," she raised her thumb showing that she just mentioned the first effect, "euphoric sensation," her index finger met her thumb for number two, " and an intense craving for me," she said. "Um, I mean, more." She added with a sheepish grin and smile. "Let's go!"

Eric slammed the rest of his warm beer, threw a twenty on the bar, and rose up to leave. He followed Sophie and Dick out of the bar and to the parking lot. The trio got into a maroon Porsche Panamera turbo. Sophie opened the back door for Eric. He climbed in and she followed close behind.

During the fifteen-minute drive, she fondled and rubbed Eric, getting him ready for upcoming action. He was more than excited and began to fondle her soft and supple breasts.

Eric woke up the next morning with a biggest hangover headache he ever had. Dick was naked and sleeping on the red leather couch. Sophie was lying on her belly in the bed next to Eric. He reached out to touch her as if not believing his sight was reality. He slowly moved his hand to reach for the small of her back and then to follow the contour of her butt cheeks.

He made small circles on her ivory skin and then gently moved his hand down to the back, upper part of her inner thigh. He could feel the moistness. He positioned his body next to hers as she moaned pleasurably in very low tones. He slid on top of her for one more go before he had to get back to his real life, a more realistic life than he had over the past twelve hours.

When he was done he kissed her on her shoulder, then on her cheek, and then quietly rolled out of the bed. He saw several unopened condom packages, a large purple vibrator, an extremely long tanned dildo, and a jar of Gun Oil lube. He cautiously tip-toed through the sexual minefield of a night past, got dressed and walked off doubting that he'd ever have a night of decadent debauchery like that again.

As he approached the elevator, he could feel a slight pain in his posterior. He reached behind to feel his butt and wondered if one of the painfully large toy made its way to his backside.

During the day he tried to recall what had happened. He really wanted to know if he was a pincushion or a pitcher during the night. After some thought, he decided that he didn't care anymore. Just then his white phone began to shake on his kitchen counter.

He went over to read the incoming text message, "HI SEXY! I enjoyed the night. Hope you enjoyed ALL of it." The message was finished with the name Dick De'Bone and had two winking faces. Eric's mind drifted to what other things may have happened during his lust-filled night. *Shit! What's he mean by the word ALL? Oh shit, did he... Hell no!*

What's it feel like to have anal sex was the search phrase he entered in the box on Google. "Shit! NO! NO! NO!" he yelled out loud to himself in the confines of his own home.

*****

"All right people, listen up. This is what we know...Jones, would you please get him caught up and in the loop to what's going on with this investigation, please? Thanks." The assistant lieutenant said to her second lead investigator, while pointing to Eric Crutchfield.

"Hey, how was your two weeks?" Detective Denise Jones asked as she opened the file on the case.

"Wow, it was great! A few nights out, many mornings sleeping-in, and a whole lot of relaxation. The vacation started off with a doozy of a night and it was two weeks trying to remember the events." He told her with a grin.

"Nice. Well, back to reality for you. Here's what we've got," he said while tossing the folder onto his oak desk while he stretched and leaned back in his chair, reminiscing about his sexual interlude of two weeks past. He escaped from his sex-filled trance, reached for the manila folder and opened it with his right hand while holding it in his left hand.

"Hmm, a decapitated vic. Okay. John Doe for now." He read further, "Okay. Yup. Found by a dog in a bag near a dumpster. Okay. I think I got it," he said to his partner. "Anything else?"

160

"Yeah, we were called about two weeks ago. In fact, I think it was three days after you left for vaca. Let's see, the guy was AIDS positive... We found two hands in the dumpster...they were in a white grocery bag," she said while flipping through her handheld note pad.

"Ya thinkin' maybe the AIDS...maybe it was a revenge killing?"

"What?"

"No, I mean, maybe someone found out he had those, but never mentioned it, and..."

"Hmm. That could be a point. I mean, it's definitely a possibility that someone could have been so pissed and enraged that they just lost it and ripped him apart."

"Let me see that picture again. Ya know, this guy looks familiar." He added while tapping his pen on his desk trying to recall if he'd ever seen the face, and if so, where it was.

Eric flipped up his laptop and went to an Internet search engine. He typed in a name and when he looked at the screen and then to the photo of the grotesque head, a cold chill came over him. He could feel his skin getting damp and he felt pale and flush.

He turned the computer to his partner. "This look like him?" he said in a nervous and shaky voice while looking straight down at the top of his desk.

"Yup!"

"Name's Dick De'Bone. He's in porn. Well, was..." he told her shyly thinking she'd immediately judge him.

"Well, that might explain the AIDS thing," she said, brushing right over any circumstantial opinions of Eric's viewing pleasure.

"Oh yeah, there's that too," he said feeling the beginning rumblings of vomit brewing in his belly. *Fuckin-A, sonofabitch, there's that too!* He took a deep breath and released it slowly.

Reaching into his pocket, Eric grabbed his cell

phone. "Hello. This is Detective Smith."

"Detective?"

"Uh yeah. Who is this?" Eric asked.

He heard a sudden click on the other end. Before he could get his phone back into his pocket, it rang.

"Hello. This is Eric," he said, trying a different approach.

"Eric. Are you a cop?"

"I am, well a detective. Who's this?"

"It's Sophie. Remember..."

"Yes. Of course. What's goin' on?" he interrupted as his mind immediately drifted to thoughts of sex.

"Uh——uh——ummm, hmmm. Well, it's like this, uh. Oh Christ, I have AIDS."

# Deep Sleep

He gave her a firm, but gentle kiss and held her tightly that night before he fell asleep. Her head rested on his shoulder while his arm held her tightly. Her supple breasts touched against his muscular chest.

"I love the way you look at me. Your big blue eyes, long full lashes, and the twinkle that shines when the light hits just right," Ben said, leaning in for more passion.

*****

"I do—n't know!" he shouted from the back room.

"You don't know because all you do is walk off every time I ask!" she yelled back to him.

The couple had been married for almost three years and it was painfully obvious that the honeymoon was over. Work, friends, life; it all took its toll.

"Look, to answer your stupid question, no. No, there's no one else, period. In fact...I...I can't even believe you'd think that. I mean, what the hell," Ben snapped. "What the hell? I'll tell ya 'what the hell'," Nicole retorted. "We don't do anything anymore. No dinners. No movies. No date night. No sex. Nada! It's all just gone!"

"What do you want from me?"

"Whaddo I want? I want a fucking husband! I want *my* fucking husband...back!" Ben was upset at the accusatory rants. He thought it was blatantly clear why the connection was gone.

It was later in the evening, but he just couldn't shake their earlier conversation. It festered.

*Honey, I really appreciate the way you point out my shortcomings...Make me feel small, insecure and unwanted.* Ben thought as he stared with extreme discontent towards his wife. *I truly love how you nitpick at every goddamn thing I do. I adore how you ignore me and consider my opinion stupid. I think it's grand that*

163

*you even point out my insecurities, while completely ignoring your own. Wait, even better, you don't think you have any issues with being insecure. You're just awesome!* He secretly flipped her his middle finger while she sat comfortably on the leather couch reading her magazine. He threw a scornful gaze and a twitch developed at the left corner of his upper lip.

Nicole would wake up early and look at her husband while he slept and wonder when he would lose his increasing belly and flabby arms. *Ya know, it'd be great if you maybe found a gym one day on your way home from work. I mean, it couldn't hurt to work out...ever! Look at ya; you've turned into a big fat pile of lazy-ass. Where the hell are those muscles you once had?*

Three years is all it took for the marriage to crumble under a roof of discord, lack of communication, and disdain. The sweet and harmonious text messages were replaced with one-word responses. The subtle sexting was replaced with flirtatious texts to others. The cute pictures of each other, in everyday situations, were gone for good. Ben wanted it all back, but he was uncertain if it was Nicole's desire too.

"Honey," Ben was shocked to hear. He could not recall the last time she had called him honey, "what happened to us?"

Even after months of thought, all he could muster was a surprised, but forlorn, "Hmm?"

"What happened? Where did our loving relationship turn? Where are *we*?" she asked.

Now, without hesitation, Ben took this line of questioning as a sign that he could let it out, "Well, we're here!" He opened his arms to express their surroundings. "And, the turn was somewhere back when you began to ignore me, or at least I felt I was ignored; think it was about six, maybe seven months ago. As for what happened, nothing. Not a damn thing. I tried. Oh, believe me, I tired! As for where we're headed...oops, you didn't ask that one, but I'll give you the answer anyway. We're headed to a big fat 'D' if we don't get this figured out now. And, yes, I'm to blame too." With that, Ben walked to his wife, grabbed her by both shoulders, pulled her close and kissed her with reckless abandon. It was his way of telling her that he wanted things to work for the better. She kissed him back.

*****

"So, Mr. and Mrs. Davis, why are you here today? the counselor asked.

"Isn't it obvious?" Nicole said with a nervous laugh.

"Well, not all couples come to see me just when problems arise. Believe it or not,
I do have many couples see me when they're looking to add more to an already stable relationship."

"Well, we're here for help. Maybe a lot...we'll see, I guess," Ben added.

"Let's get right to it then. What seems to be the issue? Ben, why don't you start?" "Work – long hours, stress – my parents, her mom, the house, and bills. Think that about covers it. Oh, and...and we talked about kids, but..."

"May I?" Nicole asked as she politely interrupted. "But, now's not a very good time to even go any further with that thought. That's probably where we both agree right now. Other than that, I think he pretty much nailed it."

"I see," the counselor said. "So, the sex life is a dud because of work and stress?
The in-laws are an added stress and there's the house and bills piled onto that? Does that sum it up?"

The couple looked at one another and almost simultaneously, "Yeah." "Yup."

"Look, I've previewed your information prior to

165

our visit. It seems to me that the work hours could be backed down a bit. Get gym memberships! Loosen up and get active! Cut back on the credit card use and the bills will fall in line. I know it sounds simple, but know this; it *is* simple. People always try to complicate things with unneeded clutter and crap. Don't do that here. You're a young couple with real issues that are easily solvable. Make sense?"

"Seems to," Nicole said as she nodded. "YES!" Ben added with a beaming smile.

*****

After a few sessions of couples counseling, the two were on track. They could both admit their inadequacies and learn from their mistakes.

"Those nails; the way they scratch me when we're having sex...manicured, deep red polished. I want you now!" Ben was on a mission and he immediately started to remove Nicky's clothes, without her resistance. The two romped for nearly an hour. It was a spectacle of aggression, reversal, and surrender. Biting, slapping, scratching, and heavy choking; they both longed for it. Later that night, while Nicky was still in bed, Ben strolled up the steps to the bedroom and plopped down next to his silent wife.

"I'm still exhausted from earlier," he mumbled while gently placing his arm around her naked body and then moved in to spoon her. Just the mere thought of her naked was usually enough for him to get in the mood. Now that he was nestled up behind her, he was over the top with excitement, no matter how tired. He rolled her over for a quickie.

A few days later, after Ben got home from work, his wife was lying in bed. He slipped in next to her for a short nap before working out. Once again his sexual energy peaked, so, as he often did, he softly rubbed her arm, letting her know his mood. After no response, he swiftly, and without warning, turned her onto her stomach.

He was quick, powerful, and in a moment it was all over. "Ever since I've been working out, my libido is in overdrive," he winked. "Oh, hold that thought," he said as the doorbell rang and he ran down the hallway.

Later that night, after a cup of tea and reading his favorite magazine, Ben was off to bed. His wife was lying down for some time already, so he was sure to be quiet while walking up the stairs and down the hall to their bedroom. He stood on his side of the bed and slowly removed his t-shirt, exposing a now buffed and chiseled chest.

He slid down his sleep-pants and slipped in under the sheet. With his nightstand light offering a slight modem of illumination, he moved his hand onto Nicole's back. "Your pale, faint, fare skin is luscious and *still* silky smooth. You turn me on. I have to have you!" he whispered into her ear while offering a slight nibble to her lobe. He knew she was out cold, but he took advantage anyway.

During their lover's session, "Your love is weird and toxic. You're pathological and no, I'm not trying to flatter you. I love the way you feel," Ben said softly while looking into her glossed over eyes, thrust after thrust.

Ben woke up disorientated and angled, like one does when he sleeps all over the bed and is uncertain of the time or place. He slept uneasily while his dreams took him to dark places. He awoke, eyes wide open, in a full sweat, clenching his teeth. He could feel the power in his lower and upper jaw contracting upon one another. He reached for his drinking water, rolled over, kissed Nicole, and drifted back to sleep.

He wasn't totally asleep, but rather in that comfortable state where he had lightning-quick and vividly short dream bursts. He dreamt of when he had met Nicole in high school, during their Senior year. He remembered how they once held hands while walking to the movies. He had dreams of the times they would sneak to the basement of her parents' home to have sex late at night. He saw, like it was real life, their sex life in photos. It zipped by very fast, as if in cover flow on a computer, and he was slinging his cursor back-and-forth at top speed.

He woke up, surprisingly refreshed and relieved at his new revelation. He leaned over and gave Nicole, lying on her side, a kiss on the outside of her shoulder. Ben got up, showered, and left for work.

He winked back to his wife, lying motionless in the bed.

His mind raced and flashed back to how it happened. He was enthralled, doing her from behind. They were in rhythm when she fell flat onto the mattress. He slid her to her side and gently added pressure to her neck. Erotic asphyxiation was a fantasy for Nicole. He added pressure with each thrust. He better understood why she died two days earlier.

## The Big Picture

Open your eyes and you shall see.
A splendid world only known to thee.
Intrigue of fiction for all to share.
Enter his world, if you dare.

## You Don't Know Jack

It was December of 1985 and Jackson Andrew Brody celebrated his sixth birthday in room 219 at Memorial General Hospital. He watched out the window as the huge snowflakes gently fell into view from the top of the glass frame and then out of view at the bottom of the pane. He stared out into the distance, past the playgrounds and big buildings, beyond the factories and silt-covered smoke stacks; he was lost.

Little Jackson didn't remember much from the accident that would change his life forever that wintery day.

His head was wrapped in bandages and a needle was in the back of his hand; the syringe held in place with clear glossy medical tape. He wasn't sure what happened to his leg, but he could only see a weird looking green and red polka-dot sock covering his toes.

The young boy tried to move his right leg, but couldn't. He made another attempt, and again, nothing. He couldn't move his foot either. He grabbed the crisp, bright white cotton sheet with his right hand and tossed it aside to find his leg in a smooth, bland and off-white plaster cast.

*****

The automobile was a mangled wreck of twisted metal and burnt debris and Jackson was the only one in the maroon Chevrolet station wagon wearing a seatbelt. The faux wood panels of the car were charred from the fire and the pigmentation of the tan front bench seat showed black scorch marks from the blaze. The steering column had been pushed up and under Edward Brody's ribs, crushing his lungs. Somehow the turn signal indicator broke off and became lodged in his chest, piercing flesh and braking bone in its path.

The paramedics said his airway filled with blood

and he suffocated within minutes. He was dead before the flames started. Mary Elizabeth Brody died instantly from severe head trauma and a displaced spinal cord after her body catapulted through the front windshield. An agile and quick-thinking EMT cut the young boy from the harness in the backseat just seconds before the first explosion created a thick, black plume of smoke that filled the cabin of the car.

The other vehicle, a burnt orange two-door Datsun, slid off the road, flipped and was nearly torn in half against a telephone pole. The disfigured driver lay lifeless on his stomach, as the freshly fallen snow soaked in the sanguine flow as it strewn from the body. The area was littered with a trail of liquor bottles and beer cans.

Jackson found out four days after the crash that both his parents had passed. Never having faced it, he wasn't exactly sure what death meant. All he knew was that his parents were never coming back and he felt alone.

Over the next fifteen years, his parents' dearest friends and Jackson's godparents, Jeff and Sharon Hammond, raised and adopted the boy. He had a full understanding of how his parents died on that day back in 1985 and he had a great disdain for alcohol, never having had any touch his lips in his twenty-one years.

It was the fall of Jackson's senior year at Harvard where he double-majored in psychology and economics, when he realized that he had an interest in international travel. The summer before his term began, he visited college friends in Germany, Belgium, Holland, and Romania. He spent the entire break soaking up diverse cultures, meeting new people, and discovering foreign lands. He wanted to continue his journeys after he graduated.

At the beginning of the new semester, the Hammond's drove him to Cambridge, Massachusetts, from the Newark area and spent the afternoon before heading home. It was just before evening and the eye-catching sunset cast low-sun hues of scarlet and yellowish brilliance, which graced the solid decks of high clouds that covered the entire sky except for a slivery-thin clear strip near the horizon. This made it difficult to see while driving.

The entire landscape took on a surreal saffron tone as the clouds reflected the fading sun's red and orange glow. The rich and vibrant fall foliage caught the light and turned the transforming leaves into spectacular shades of deep reds, vivid greens, and glowing yellows. The entire landscape took on a vibrancy.

The low light combined with the tree-lined streets drew shadows throughout the entire area, which made driving difficult. After an early dinner, the Hammond's dropped their son at the grand, stone-arched walkway to his dorm building and drove off on their drive back to New Jersey.

On campus, students flowed freely, walking from rooms to class buildings and crossing streets without hesitation. Excellent traffic control kept four-wheeled dangers at ease. Jackson saw a friend and chatted briefly before walking down the long, brick paved path. The two discussed their upcoming class schedules and made arrangements to meet later in the library.

As he turned, shifted his weight, and placed his left foot towards his temporary college home, he heard the wretched, spine-tingling sound of screeching rubber tires skidding on cement combined with the blaring scream of a car horn. He stopped in his tracks and then heard the colossal impact and horrifying clanging of metal-on-metal of cars crashing together. Jackson ran down to the small intersection where he viewed the still smoking aftermath of the wreck.

He stopped when he saw the mutilated wreckage of the pewter, stodgy Buick Century nearly split in half as if a missile had hit it. He could see Sharon's rumpled, lifeless body lying on the ground, up against a tree. He ran to her and she had no pulse and her head was a maimed and bloody mess. She was gone.

As he made his way to the car, he could see Jeff. It looked like he was trapped between the dashboard and the seat. When Jackson got closer he could see Jeff's legs were severed near mid-thigh. The industrial plastic bottom of the dash had cut clean through. His eyes were wide open and his face was already pale and blue. Jackson reached inside and Jeff was dead too. "Call an ambulance now goddammit!" He yelled to a stunned and frozen bystander.

Jackson walked over to the red Nissan 300ZX to see the man behind the wheel gasping for his next breath. Not sure exactly what had happened, Jackson spoke before he could even smell the alcohol. "Hold still buddy. Help is on the way," he shouted. He could easily surmise that the driver was the only one wearing a seatbelt. Moments later the medics had the man pulled from his car and in the back of the ambulance.

The police officer on the scene could tell immediately what had happened. It took a few minutes of standing, pausing, and viewing the scene before Jackson had figured it out too. The sheer ferocity of the impact and displacement of the vehicles clearly showed that the Nissan was traveling at a high-rate when it blew through the stop sign and t- boned the Hammond's automobile.

Jackson's memory went back to what he knew about the accident that took his parents. Although he couldn't recall specific events other than the initial sounds and being cut from the car, he could vividly remember how it felt to lose his family. He immediately felt the twisted torment, the agonizing pain, the true denial, and mostly, the anger.

It was that ire that transcended Jackson to a place of

darkness and vehement displeasure. In a blur, the lectures and studying of psychology principles and applications ran through his head almost as fast as speed-reading. The thought of analyzing his feelings were far in the distance of his mind.

He didn't care to examine the inner reaches of his psyche or determine the essence of his anguish. All he wanted was to alleviate the emotional fury of his rage. Jackson slowly walked past the long black station wagon marked, *Coroner* in thin, bold, cursive white lettering and with the back swing-door open, he could see the motionless figures of Jeff and Sharon zipped in the confines of the lightweight, white body bags. Pausing only briefly, he continued on his way to the ambulance.

"My parents died in a crash. My godparents just died in a crash, but the drunken asshole that ran the stop sign somehow survived. Great. That's just fuckin' great!" He mumbled it to himself, as he could feel his pulse quicken and watched as his right fist clenched, squeezing the anger. He took a few deep breaths to release his building frustration.

Jackson didn't see any of the emergency medical technicians near or in the ambulance. He peered around the closed back door and stuck his head inside the opening of the second swinging door to see the offending driver lying on a metal gurney covered with a pure white sheet, neatly pulled up to his waist.

He was bare-chested with small spots of blood on his flesh. The EMT had hooked the patient up to an intravenous drip system to instantly deliver fluids and pain medication. Jackson looked around, grabbed the edge of the closed door, and stepped into the back of the vehicle.

He felt as though he was stuck to the ceiling of the ambulance looking down on the entire events as they unfolded in slow motion. "What's your name?" Jackson asked the man in a soft and pleasant voice.

Short on breath and struggling as it was, the man could only mutter a barely understandable, "C...C...Cu...Cur..."

"Curt?" Jackson asked, looking over his shoulder to the outside, as the man gargled the last attempt. The driver of the red Nissan ZX only nodded his head in approval.

It wasn't a negotiation. He expertly slipped one of the purple nitrile gloves on his right hand, pulling it down to his wrist until it made a snapping sound. He took his left hand and squeezed the air out of the glove by interlocking his hands until he felt comfortable it was skintight.

He knelt beside the man on the gurney, peeked out of the back of the ambulance and then looked back at the man. Jackson showed no emotion, no pain, and no caring as he looked into Curt's eyes and deep into his soul. He suddenly felt a surging tidal wave of solitary peace and tranquility wash over him.

He placed his hand over the mouth of the drunkard, being careful to tightly pinch the nose with his thumb and forefinger, and only removed his hand when he felt the violent shaking and struggling stop. It didn't take nearly as long as he had imagined it would. There was no more breath. There was no more life. The twitching was gone. He was unwavering in his decision as he slipped the glove into his jean pocket, hopped out of the ambulance, and walked off into the moonlit night.

Any emotion Jackson had left him that cold, autumn night in September and it would prove good for his future endeavors. On that eve, Jackson Andrew Hammond- Brody simply became... Jack Brody.

About the author:

Christopher Winterberg is a new author. He has not been published in any reviews, quarterlies, journals, periodicals, or elsewhere. He has never won a young writers award, middle-aged writers award, or an old writers award. Never having been labeled as one of the most famous writers of any generation, era, or century, he has received zero literary awards. He does, however, look forward to those in the future, if warranted. You can find out more about Christopher at chriswinterberg.com.

Christopher has not appeared at any book events, festivals, conferences, or even book signings. Okay, maybe one. He looks forward to more in the future, as well. He is, however, a member of a writing group, which he attends sporadically. He is not internationally or nationally known. His first book has recently been published.

If you're daring and wish to, you may contact Christopher Winterberg either through a post on his website, or at info@chriswinterberg.com